"No, that's not po⋯
blood relatives six⋯
and no one came forward. I even went to
Texas and asked Emma's grandfather to
take Emma. I begged him, and the man
turned us away. He lost his chance. She's
mine, Dad. Emma is mine." Panic rose in
her chest.

"Please tell me Henry has a plan and that no one
can take her from me, especially not some distant
relative looking for a payout."

Emma's guardianship had come with four hundred
thousand dollars from her father's SGLI—the
military life insurance paid out after Liam's
backpack and gear were found burned near an
outpost, changing his status from MIA to KIA.
Emma's paternal grandfather had added a hundred
grand to the pot when he had signed over his rights
to the child. Kelsey hadn't needed the money, so she
put all of it into Emma's trust fund for when she
became an adult. Like hell someone was going to
use Emma to snatch it up.

"It's not a distant relative. It's her father, Kelsey.
He's been found alive and he wants to meet his
daughter."

Dear Reader,

I'm so pleased you picked up a copy of
*Brought Together by His Baby*. I hope you love
Mercy Hospital and its staff as much as I enjoyed
writing the drama of their lifesaving efforts and the
challenges of falling in love amid the bustle
and glamor of LA.

Kelsey is an ob-gyn to the Hollywood elite at Mercy,
where she also runs a charity for moms who can't
afford good care. I worked on military bases in
Hawaii and California that were run by incredible
volunteers like Kelsey, and I wanted to share a few
of their stories, albeit in a medical setting. I hope
I've captured them in Kelsey's strong, dedicated
character.

My time working with service members also
allowed me to dive into the drama of Liam's escape
and reintegration into the medical world as he
heals. He's one of my favorite heroes—how can
anyone resist a sexy military medic as he dotes on
his baby girl? But is he ready for both fatherhood
and a new, fulfilling relationship with Kelsey?

Welcome to Mercy—stay awhile and you just might
fall in love, too!

XO,

*Kristine Lynn*

# BROUGHT TOGETHER BY HIS BABY

KRISTINE LYNN

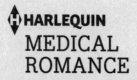

HARLEQUIN

MEDICAL
ROMANCE

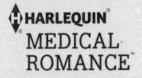

**HARLEQUIN**®
**MEDICAL**
**ROMANCE**™

Recycling programs
for this product may
not exist in your area.

ISBN-13: 978-1-335-59491-4

Brought Together by His Baby

Harlequin Enterprises ULC
22 Adelaide St. West, 41st Floor
Toronto, Ontario M5H 4E3, Canada
www.Harlequin.com

**Printed in U.S.A.**

Hopelessly addicted to espresso and HEAs, **Kristine Lynn** pens high-stakes contemporary romances in the wee morning hours before teaching writing at an Arizona university. Luckily, the stakes there aren't as dire. When she's not grading, writing or searching for the perfect vanilla latte, she can be found on the hiking trails behind her home with her daughter and puppy. She'd love to connect on Twitter, Instagram or Facebook.

*Brought Together by His Baby*

is Kristine Lynn's debut title for Harlequin.

Visit the Author Profile page at Harlequin.com.

# CHAPTER ONE

KELSEY GAINES SQUEEZED her eyes tighter.

*Leave me alone*, she willed. *Please.*

But the images swooped in anyway—pale reminders of her worst moments set to the soundtrack of Page screaming in agony. The sensation that Kelsey could have done something—*should* have done something as a physician and Page's friend—was a ghost pain that seized her chest.

She struggled to breathe as the memories assaulted her.

So much blood. An infant not breathing. CPR performed on the small body until a wail filled the room. Then the steady beep of a machine marking the infant an orphan…

Kelsey wrenched open her eyes and checked her phone. Eleven minutes past three a.m. It was safe to say sleep was off the table for the rest of the night.

Sighing, she pulled on the pair of stained sweatpants dangling off the edge of the king sleigh bed and downed the lukewarm water on her nightstand in one gulp. But the hangover of the nightmare remained on her chilled skin.

*You didn't kill Page*, the part of her brain desperate for sleep tried to tell her.

That was only partially true.

Page's death might not have happened on her operating table, but *Kelsey* had talked Page into resigning from the Gold Fleece Foundation. Doing so allowed the Foundation to cover her delivery when her estranged husband had filed for divorce and then been declared missing from his military outpost. After all, Kelsey's charity had been designed with women like Page in mind—those who didn't have family or funds to support them during the biggest moment of their lives.

*She* had recommended that obstetrician from Santa Barbara because her treating Page, a Mercy Hospital nurse and former Gold Fleece board member, also a friend, would have been a conflict of interest. And because Kelsey had let go of control for that *one* day her best friend had paid a terrible price.

The ghost pain returned, squeezing Kelsey's lungs. Kelsey might have lost a friend, and Emma her mother. But Page had lost her *life*.

Thirty-five years after losing her mother to the same complication, Page's death had been another reminder why Kelsey had to keep control at all times: in the OR, in her practice, at the Foundation.

And with Emma.

When shrill cries rang out in the next room the infantile sirens of warning flooded Kelsey with purpose. She jumped out of bed, the cool tiled floor beneath her feet acting like a jolt of caffeine.

*Emma. My sweet baby.*

Well, almost. Just one more set of papers to sign before her guardianship was official.

Kelsey smiled weakly, recalling the first few lines of the letter that had changed both their lives.

*If you're reading this, then the worst has happened and you're all I have left. Which means... you're all Emma has left. Please take care of my baby girl. Our baby girl.*

Of course Kelsey would—every day for the rest of her life. Even though it had meant losing Dex, who'd disappeared like June fog on a hot July day when Child Services had brought Emma to their house. He'd been crystal-clear about never wanting kids, but if Kelsey hadn't stepped in Emma would have ended up in foster care. Not a chance was that happening on Kelsey's watch.

Dex breaking up with her had hurt, but not enough to change her mind.

When she turned on the light, the crystals from the chandelier sparkled against the walls, making the sepulchral space seem almost regal. *If only.* Royalty would have staff to help out on nights like this.

Kelsey shuddered through a half-yawn as she threw on a robe. Therein lay the conundrum that kept her up on the nights when the nightmares didn't.

As impossible as this life was—balancing her career as an OB to the Hollywood elite with single parenting—how could she wish away something as precious as time with Emma? She was Kelsey's chance to get things right, to be the kind of mother Kelsey wished she'd had.

But that didn't mean it wasn't hard.

Kelsey's father hadn't been shy to chime in. *"That's parenting. Wish I could tell you it gets easier, but I'm not one for fibbing."*

Emma screeched again.

*You weren't kidding, Dad.*

"I'm coming, sweetie. I'm coming."

Kelsey shuffled into the kitchen and turned on the bottle warmer, placing a premade bottle inside as she succumbed to another yawn. Some sleep would be nice. Her dad had argued it was time to hire a nanny. She could afford it and, frankly, she couldn't afford not to where her career was concerned. But who could she trust enough with her child? No, better to let Emma stay in the hospital daycare, where Kelsey could keep an eye on her.

With the hospital on her mind, Kelsey ran through her morning appointments while she waited for the bottle to heat up.

An eight a.m. high-risk delivery, followed by consults, and then a Gold Fleece Foundation board meeting to welcome Page's replacement. Anxiety crawled over Kelsey's skin. Once the new member signed a contract, it would be official. Page's stamp on the Foundation—and on Kelsey's life—would only be a memory.

*Focus on the delivery. You know what to do.*

If it were up to her, she'd start with a Cesarean, since it was likely to end up that way.

*But it isn't up to me—not entirely.*

Her young patient's plans to have cameras in the room took precedence over Kelsey's own professional instinct and experience, since the birth was to be live streamed for the mom's six million social media followers. Still, breech was breech, and short of a miracle—which Kelsey was running dangerously low on these past six months—surgery was inevitable. If that occurred, the film crew would have to leave. Kelsey had made sure the mother-to-be knew that at their last checkup.

Either way, she was in for a long day at the office.

When the warmer turned itself off, Kelsey shook the bottle, then sprinkled the inside of her arm with the formula to make sure it wasn't too hot before heading back to her daughter's room. *Her daughter.* It hadn't sunk in. After years of waiting for Dex to change his mind about marriage and kids, and years of guilt over her own birth causing her mother's death, Kelsey had a child of her own and clarity where her dead-end relationship was concerned. All while her career thrived.

She stood in the doorway for half a moment, letting gratitude and grief wash over her in equal torrents.

"Oh, Emma. I wouldn't trade you in my life for anything except your mother being back here with us," she whispered. "One thing is for certain—I'm never letting another person I love out of my care."

The risks were just too great.

The moon glittered off the ocean below, but it was otherwise a starless night. Despite the warmth enveloping Kelsey's skin, she felt a shiver run down her spine.

She swooped in and picked up the rosy-cheeked infant and Emma's screams relaxed into soft mewls of hunger.

"Hey, there, little miss. I'm here. No need to bring down the house. We get to see Grandpa's friend Henry today. He's the lawyer that's going to help us become a family."

She'd hoped to squeeze in the final guardianship paperwork before her morning delivery, but at this rate she'd need the sleep. What was a few hours when forever stretched in front of them?

Emma cooed in response to the bottle Kelsey brandished, then giggled as the warmed formula reached her lips. Kelsey relished the love emanating from the child. She smoothed the errant hairs off Emma's forehead and kissed it, imprinting this moment into her memories.

"You're everything I ever wanted," she whispered against the soft skin of Emma's cheeks.

Emma just continued suckling away at her bottle, her eyes barely open.

Kelsey fought back another yawn. "You're also the only thing keeping me together."

Just as Emma drifted off to sleep Kelsey's phone rang, sharp and shrill in the otherwise silent kitchen. Emma released the bottle and started wailing again.

"Shh…shh… It's okay, hun…"

Kelsey maneuvered the nipple past the baby's trembling bottom lip and got her feeding again before she turned her wrath on her phone. She never silenced it at night, in case a patient had gone into labor, but she sorely regretted it at that moment.

Her frown only deepened when she saw her father's number on the caller ID.

"What's wrong?" she asked, in lieu of a more traditional greeting.

"Did I wake you?" asked Mike Gaines.

"No. I was up."

"The nightmares again, hmm?"

"Maybe… Yeah. But I'm handling them. How did you know?"

"You're my daughter. I know you better than anyone."

That was true. Her dad was one of her best friends—her only friend now that Dex had left and Page had…

Kelsey shuddered. "You didn't answer my question. What's happened, Dad?"

He paused before continuing, and when he did his voice had lost the calm it usually carried. "You know I think of Emma like my granddaughter already, right?"

Kelsey swallowed back the wave of emotion that rose in her throat, sticky and hot.

"Mmm-hmm," she answered.

"And I wouldn't ever willingly let anything happen to either of you?"

"I know. Dad, you're scaring me. What's this about?"

Emma sucked away at her bottle, her eyes shut, her body relaxed in Kelsey's arms. Love washed through Kelsey every time she looked at her daughter. But now the love was tainted with worry.

Mike sighed. "There's a problem with your guardianship. I just heard from Henry."

If it were biologically possible for Kelsey's cells to freeze one by one, seizing her breath, that was what happened.

"But he said it was fine. I'm supposed to meet him this morning to sign the last of the documents."

"I know. Which is why I'm calling."

"The letter from Page should have been enough—"

The last half of her thought was swallowed by fear.

"It was, hun. It was. Gosh, I'm sorry to have to tell you this, but I didn't want you to hear it from anyone else." He paused, and the air was pregnant with foreboding. "A blood relative reached out to claim custody."

Kelsey shook her head, even though her dad couldn't see her. "No, that's not possible. The court gave any blood relatives sixty days to contact them and no one came forward. I even went to Texas and asked Emma's grandfather to take her. I *begged* him, and the man turned us away. He lost his chance. She's mine, Dad. Emma is *mine*."

Panic rose in her chest and no amount of self-determination could will it back into the pit of her stomach.

"Please tell me Henry has a plan and that no one can take her from me—especially not some distant relative looking for a payout."

Emma's guardianship would come with four hundred thousand dollars from her father Liam's SGLI—the military life insurance paid out after his rucksack and gear had been found burned near an enemy outpost, changing his status from MIA to KIA. Emma's paternal grandfather had added a hundred grand to the pot when he had signed over his rights to the child. Kelsey didn't need the money, so she'd put all of it into a trust fund for when Emma became an adult. Like hell someone was going to use Emma to snatch it up.

"It's not a distant relative. It's her father, Kelsey. He's been found alive and he wants to meet his daughter."

Kelsey's thoughts spun like an out-of-control carousel while she paced the floor with Emma on her hip. The child giggled, clapping her hands in glee each time Kelsey spun and headed back in the other direction.

What Kelsey wouldn't do to protect that giggle at all costs.

*My God*, she thought. *Liam Everson is alive.*

All the scenarios she'd run through her head and that one had never occurred to her.

Kelsey knew a little about him from the three years since Page had lived in California. She and Liam had been estranged, so he'd remained in Texas while Page took a job as a nurse at Mercy, and then joined the Gold Fleece Foundation board after her first year. Liam had been an Army trauma doc.

He and Page had tried to reconcile before his last deployment, and even though the reconciliation hadn't worked Page had found out she was pregnant just days after Liam deployed again. Neither had expected the baby, but both had been in agreement about one thing—they'd do anything to make sure the life growing inside Page didn't know anything but love.

They'd been going to work on a joint custody agreement when Liam returned, but then he'd been captured and everything had changed with that one devastating call.

And now he was safe and home on American soil…and his daughter was in Kelsey's arms.

On one hand, this was a miracle.

A miracle that Page would miss.

But on the other hand…*oh, God*…it was a miracle that might sever Kelsey's connection to Emma.

*No.*

"Can he take her, Dad?"

"I dunno, hun. Henry said he'll get in touch when he knows more. Right now, it just sounds like the guy wants to meet his daughter. But he's stationed in Texas, so I'm not sure how that'll work."

"But how will he care for her if he's in the Army? He deploys every year," Kelsey said, her voice dangerously close to shrill.

An hour had passed since she got the news, willing it to be a bad joke of some kind.

"Kelsey, I know you're reeling. We all are. But you need to hear Henry out. He's concerned that how we handle this might make or break your career. Page was part of the Foundation, and that's gonna come up at some point if Emma's dad makes a custody play."

Kelsey barked out a humorless laugh. "I don't care about my *career.* I care about *Emma.*"

"No one's questioning your love for the child—but Kels, listen to reason. Captain Everson is her *father.* And he's just escaped a war-torn country by trekking eighty miles to a sovereign nation. After a month of hiding and being on the run he's been home two months, processing the worst news a soldier can get—the mother of the child he hasn't even met *died,* Kelsey."

Kelsey's breath came in short gasps. She gulped for more oxygen, but every time she inhaled it felt like she sucked in water, not air. She was drowning on dry land.

"I know," she whispered. "I knew it the minute you told me who contacted Henry. But that doesn't mean I don't count, right? I mean, I've raised Emma for the past six months, Dad. Six months of doctor's appointments, daycare interviews, nighttime bottle feedings, diapers…"

She trailed off and kissed Emma's head, where her baby-fine hairs were finally beginning to grow out. Emma smelled like the sun and soap and love. She smelled like home.

"You count, yes. But you can't deny a soldier—heck, any man, for that matter—his chance to know his daughter."

*Of course I can't. But I can't just stand idly by and watch fate take her from me, either.*

"What about the letter from Page? She was my best friend and her letter said I was her choice for Emma."

She was on the verge of screaming…tearing her hair out. This wasn't how this was supposed to go. She wasn't supposed to work harder than anyone she knew and do the right thing only to have everything spin out of control in the end.

"Don't I at least have a say in what happens to her?"

"Don't think I don't agree with you," her father said.

The unmistakable crack in his voice was enough

for her to consider running away to a country with no extradition treaty, with him and Emma in tow.

"But it isn't up to us. The choice Page made was an impossible one, but she did it thinking she was out of options. And, like it or not, Bug, an option has presented itself. For now, just think of this as a blessing on Emma's behalf. She has a father who's alive and who wants to be part of her life."

"Okay…"

Kelsey choked back a sob and kissed Emma's forehead, leaving tears behind. She wiped them off and concentrated on loving this infant until someone forced her to stop. It was the only thing she controlled at that moment. It was her lifeline.

"And I know it hurts to imagine what that'll mean for you—trust me, I'm scared to death I'll miss seeing the girl grow up too—but this is good news, Kels."

*Good news that would explode her life into unrecognizable shards.*

"I can't imagine not waking up to her every night…every morning."

Had she really just complained about the three-a.m. wake-up? Even now, she couldn't recall anything before taking Emma into her home and her heart.

"What if I miss her first steps? Her first word?"

*What if something happens to Emma when I'm not there to protect her?*

Kelsey's knees trembled under the weight of the

news and she slumped into an overstuffed arm-chair. Emma curled against her neck, her breath hot on Kelsey's skin.

"Why don't I come by at seven-thirty and we can make a plan? It'll gimme a chance to chat with Henry and see if there's any more details before Emma's father heads your way."

"He's coming *here*? Today? I'm losing Emma right now?" Panic flooded Kelsey's system.

"No one's losing anything, hun. He's just coming to meet you. To meet her."

Kelsey hissed out a breath, but none of the pressure behind her eyes dissipated.

"Kels…" her dad said softly. His voice betrayed the concern he usually kept at bay.

"I'll be fine."

"I don't doubt you will be. But there's one more thing."

The floor might as well have dropped out from beneath Kelsey's feet the way her stomach lurched.

"There's more?"

What else could there possibly be?

"Nothing crazy. Just something Henry said in passing that I thought you should know before you meet the guy. I'm not sure if Page ever said anything, but his father is the founder and president of—"

"I know who he is. You can't work in healthcare and not know the Eversons. But what does that have to do with Emma?" Kelsey asked, bordering on hysteria.

"Henry seems to think they'll have the full weight of Everson Health Systems to throw behind a custody case if Captain Everson decides to open one."

Kelsey's hands shook.

"Not that he's planning to, as far as we know, but Henry wants to cover all bases just in case."

"They don't get to do that. Liam's dad refused to take custody six months ago, right? I mean, there's a signed court document."

"I'm not sure… Henry just wanted you to know, but you can't let it worry you, okay?"

"Stop. Just…stop, please. I love you, Dad, and I'm grateful for the call, but I can't take in anything else right now."

"Lemme just say this. The man's her father, and when I say that it's with love and empathy for what you're going through, but if I were in his position I'd move heaven and earth to get to you, hun."

Kelsey set Emma on the *Very Hungry Caterpillar* play mat in front of her and gazed around the room. A year ago it had been decorated by the renowned designer Christian Milan himself, and then featured on the cover of *Vogue* along with Kelsey in her doctor's coat over a power suit. Now Kelsey was slumped on her laundry-covered couch in brandless spit-up-stained sweats and her boho carpet was buried somewhere beneath the eighty-four kids' toys strewn about the room.

Her life was unrecognizable.

But she *loved* it.

Emma had completed a part of her life Kelsey hadn't realized was missing. Being with the child was what she looked forward to most, aside from helping other women realize their dreams of motherhood.

Grief sat square on her temple, giving her a tension headache.

"I need to get some rest, Dad. I'll see you at seven-thirty."

"Sure thing, Kels. Rest will help. I promise everything will look better in the morning. Henry told me that a few decades ago and look how that turned out. You're the best part of my life, kiddo."

Kelsey winced. She didn't need a reminder that she'd made the man a widower.

"Thanks, Dad. Talk to you soon."

She hung up the phone and picked Emma up off the floor, tucking the half-coo, half-giggle noise the baby made into her heart while she put Emma back to bed.

Alone in her room, she pulled up a news video of Liam's emotional return on her phone. Kelsey recognized his chiseled features from a photo Page had had. Despite the overgrown beard and long, scraggly hair, she caught a glimpse of a warrior.

A warrior she might be up against in the battle of her life.

She replayed the video twice more, looking for clues. Why had he waited so long to find Emma, though? He'd been home two months now.

Kelsey sank into a rocker identical to the one she had in the living room. She found a soft knitted blanket and wrapped it around her torso. Tears slid hot and heavy down her cheeks, dappling her gray sweatshirt with yet another liquid substance.

She wasn't guaranteed another minute of time with the beautiful child she'd come to love as her own. Her future was up in the air and she didn't like the unease that caused. She needed rest—but more than that, she needed to attack this new development head-on.

*Captain Liam Everson.*

She couldn't fight the fact that he was Emma's father, nor the obvious reason he'd been unable to claim his rights until now. But Kelsey deserved to be a part of Emma's life too—as a physician who delivered babies safely every day, who was in a better position than her to protect her?

With a new sense of purpose, Kelsey strode to her closet. She unbuttoned and slipped out of the fear cloaking her, shelved the anxiety draped around her shoulders, and picked out a suit to replace them both. If Liam Everson, the warrior, was coming here, she'd be ready to do battle for what mattered most.

# CHAPTER TWO

LIAM STARED AT the tall, ornately decorated door and ran his hand through his hair. Man, the new cut felt good. It reminded him of who he had been before…well, just *before*.

Everything in his life was going to sit on one side of a line now, wasn't it?

Before his capture, and after.

Before he'd left Page alone, at the beginning of a high-risk pregnancy, their divorce papers still sitting on his kitchen counter.

And after…

That particular "after" had gotten him through the worst eight months of his life—knowing he'd get to come home to his baby. And it—rather, *she*—had a name, too. *Emma Lynn.*

"You've got this, buddy. You've done the work. Now's the fun part. You get to meet your daughter," he whispered under his breath.

The worry that the work wouldn't be enough, that he'd see his daughter and not feel anything, poked its head from behind visceral memories of his own childhood, which had been laced with neglect. But that was all it was, right—a worry. Because he'd been raised by the most selfish man in Texas—well, top five, at least…he couldn't be sure.

Looking up at the home where his daughter had

lived these past six months, a grin spread across his face.

He hadn't even met her yet and his world revolved around her. He wasn't his dad and never would be.

*It's been a long time coming, but you've earned this.*

Liam knocked harder than he had the first time, but stopped short of ringing the bell in case Emma was napping. Still nothing. Huh? Was anyone home?

His nerves showed in the small half-moon semicircles he'd dug into his palms with nails that were still too long. *Damn.* He should have cut them so he didn't scratch Emma when he held her.

He needed to trust his process; he'd waited to meet his daughter until he was ready. And now he was. He'd done two months of work to ensure a lifetime of building a healthy relationship with Emma.

It was all he'd thought about as his plane—a private flight to L.A., so he could avoid the media coverage that had tracked his return to the States—had soared over the open fields and canyons of his home state, giving way to the deeper reds and browns of Arizona, and then finally touched down with cerulean waves off to his left.

He might have hated the place where he'd been born and raised once, but not anymore. It would be the first time he felt like he was going home when he arrived back in Texas with his daughter.

He repeated the three-pronged mantra he'd taught the trauma docs at Walter Reed Army Medical Center: *Calm body, measured breaths, focused mind.*

"We did tell them noon, right?" asked Nancy, his mediator, tapping her feet.

"We did."

He winced as she rang the doorbell twice in quick succession. He hadn't wanted to hire anyone—especially not the sharpshooter Nancy was turning out to be—but his boss, Major Peters, had insisted.

*"If you're not going to file for full custody now, then at least cover your backside in case you do."*

Liam wasn't sure that was the right decision—after all, Page had chosen this woman Kelsey for a reason. Showing up with a court official was sure to start them off on the wrong foot—something he'd waited two months precisely to avoid. But he agreed with his boss on one point—he was Emma's father and he'd be taking that role seriously. With a job lined up in Austin, he'd be able to do that and officially leave deployments behind to be there for his daughter.

"Ugh! Is no one on time anymore?" Nancy glanced at her watch and scowled.

"Let's just give her a second," Liam said. "She's taken care of Emma for six months. She's earned some time to wrap her head around this."

Nancy nodded, her eyes focused. "You're right.

We should take a breath and be patient. We're playing the long game here."

*This isn't a game*, he wanted to tell her. *It's my family, my future.*

Liam's skin tingled but he nodded.

*Measured breaths.*

This might be Nancy's first official act as his mediator, but it would be her last, too. He needed a champion in his corner, rooting for him as he tried to be the best dad he could, not a sniper shooting at the crowd from a closed window.

Liam rocked back on his heels and glanced over the modern facade of the massive house. The entrance in front of them might as well be a doorway to another universe, it was so different from the world he'd cultivated for himself.

For a moment he questioned his decision to come. Emma wouldn't want for anything here, if the chandelier he could see through the glass above the door was any indication of the resources this woman had. But he'd left a similar life intentionally. Money didn't mean love.

He inhaled sharply.

*Calm body.*

His father was proof of that. All the money in the world and he'd turned down his own granddaughter because he was "done raising kids and, to be frank, I wasn't very fond of it the first time around."

It was on Liam now to fix those mistakes, and he knew he wouldn't ever make the same ones his father had. He was *choosing* Emma and he'd never let her feel otherwise.

"Are you sure you don't want me to file custody paperwork? This is *your* daughter, Mr. Everson, not hers."

"I'm sure. And Mr. Everson is my father. Call me Liam, please."

He set his jaw, felt a small muscle in his cheek pulsing under the stress wafting from Nancy like cheap cologne.

*Focused mind.*

"A custody judge would favor you," Nancy insisted.

"Please. That's not on the table right now."

Nancy opened her mouth like she wanted to contest again, but Liam shook his head.

"Emma is all that's got me through the past eight months…knowing I'd get to meet her. Not under these circumstances, necessarily, but still, to finally hold her. That's all I want."

A lump formed in his throat. It was made of loss and bound in hope. He coughed until it loosened and sank back down to his stomach.

"Whatever comes next, Ms. Gaines and I will decide together."

She could fly to him—or vice versa. He wasn't opposed to her visiting Emma…not after all she'd done to keep his daughter safe. They could handle this without lawyers.

He rapped hard on the door again.

"Fine. But Liam…?"

"Yeah?"

"Be wary of Ms. Gaines. Regardless of what you think of this doctor, she's legally almost Emma's guardian. The last thing we want to do is scare her into fighting back."

Liam clamped down on the inside of his cheek, releasing it when the taste of iron swirled along his tongue. He didn't have any feelings for Kelsey Gaines one way or another, aside from gratefulness. It would be a lot harder to take over as Emma's father if she'd been sent to foster care. Besides, what Page had said about her boss painted a picture of a kind, reasonable woman.

"Got it. Thanks, Nancy."

His tone was kind, even though in the back of his head he'd already drafted an email to Nancy, relieving her of her position. He'd type it out and send it that afternoon.

He rang the doorbell again, gritting his teeth. He didn't want to, but they couldn't wait out there forever.

The door opened and a stern face appeared. A stern, self-assured, *stunning* face.

*This is Dr. Gaines?*

Liam stepped back and took her in, assessing the image against what he knew about her.

Kelsey Gaines was supposedly rich. Like, filthy private-jet-and-pilot rich. She ran her own OB-GYN practice that almost exclusively catered to the

Hollywood elite, so she was practically a household name around here. Every glossy magazine photo of her showed a successful and beautiful woman, if not overly made up.

*Yeah, that tracks.*

She wore a sharp black pant suit with a deep V-necked jade blouse. He swallowed hard. A slicked-back ponytail and severe dark make-up completed the look. But the photos hadn't done her a damn bit of justice. This woman could run a *country*.

Then there were her eyes…flashing green eyes set in a flawless olive complexion. They bored into his, then raked over his body like a scalpel's edge, ready to cut him. Damn, they were unnerving.

"Captain Everson."

The words sounded like part of a curse. It hadn't been a question, but he nodded.

"Sorry. I was feeding Emma."

*Dressed like that?*

"Kelsey Gaines, right? Nice to meet you."

He stuck out a hand but she didn't take it. His guard went up as he let the lapse in formality slide. He'd gotten the impression from Page that the woman his late wife had worked for was kind and effusive. At first impression, she was neither.

"*Dr.* Gaines. But, yes. It's a pleasure."

Her words said one thing, but the scowl on her face said otherwise.

"Sorry. Dr. Gaines, this is Nancy Thomas. She's

just here to observe." It seemed important to share the latter, since Dr. Gaines didn't seem particularly thrilled they were there. "May we come in?"

"Nice to meet you, Ms. Thomas. Please come in—and pardon my tardiness. Emma comes first, always."

Her words were syrupy sweet and Nancy lapped them up.

Okay, so it was *him* Dr. Gaines didn't care for. He winced. If Page had written to him about the woman she'd worked with for the past three years, she'd probably told Dr. Gaines about him. Or the version of him that had led to his and Page's separation.

*But I'm not that guy anymore.*

The words sat stale on his tongue.

"Thanks for having us on such short notice," he said. He bit back a grin when she stepped on a rogue plush elephant that let out a soft squeak. "I guess being a parent and full-time doctor doesn't leave much time for yourself."

He avoided looking at the myriad photos of Emma hung like landmines around the entrance-way. Each one tugged at his heartstrings.

"Actually, we manage just fine. My father moved to a place in the grounds of my property and he helps out with Emma while I work. When he can't, the hospital daycare is available, and it is the best in the county. Thank you for your concern, though," she said. "I may not come from quite the medical stock you do, but I can balance more than you think."

Her eyes had turned to seafoam-green icicles, capable of killing a man with a single look.

She turned back to the stairs and began to climb them.

His brows rose in appreciation. She could hold her own. He'd have been impressed if she hadn't been treating him like an adversary instead of someone who also cared about Emma.

"I'm sure you can. But still, thanks. This means a lot."

*Everything*, his heart corrected. *It means everything.*

Dr. Gaines paused in front of white double doors, and when she turned back to him her eyes had turned to liquid emeralds. His pulse sped up, but he inhaled deeply until it regulated itself.

*Measured breaths, Cap. Get it together.*

"I want you to know how much I love the little girl in there," she whispered. "You may be her flesh and blood, Captain Everson, but I'm her mother. That won't change, no matter what happens here today."

Liam felt the blow like he'd been physically kicked in the chest.

He'd counted on the emotional heft it would take to meet Emma, to know Page wouldn't be there. But he'd underestimated the claim Emma's guardian would make on his daughter. And the way she would snake past his defenses.

"I won't argue that fact. And if I haven't been clear about my feelings, I want you to know I'm beyond grateful she's had you in her life, Dr. Gaines. I'm just here to meet my daughter and work out a plan for her care going forward," he said.

That seemed to do the trick. "Call me Kelsey," she said.

He nodded as Kelsey pushed open the doors and revealed an eight-hundred-square-foot suite decorated from wall to wall with zoo animals and more plush stuffed toys for a baby to engage with. It was...*perfect*. Just what he'd do if—no, *when* he was given the chance.

His chest pulsed with the loss of being robbed of his daughter's first six months.

He moved past Kelsey into the space and, as if pulled by a force greater than his own will, made his way to the crib. He closed his eyes against the pressure that had built behind his lids but when he opened them again and laid eyes on the soft, pale skin of the child he and Page had created out of what had been left of their love, the tears fell.

He reached down and scooped Emma into his arms. Her soft warmth melted his defenses, and when she cooed against his chest the heat spread through his limbs. As if by magic, all the stress, the danger, the hiding from those bent on killing him—all of it evaporated.

A deep, all-encompassing love filled the places carved out by grief and it was suddenly crystal-clear what needed to happen.

He turned to Kelsey, Emma's heartbeat steadying his resolve.

"Can we talk?" he asked.

Liam temporarily lost his nerve somewhere between Kelsey's jade-green eyes turning to stethoscope-sized saucers and her glossy lips parting just enough to draw his focus. He'd scared her, but he couldn't think about that. The moment Emma's small hand wrapped around his thumb he'd been *hers*, wholly and completely. Which meant he couldn't go home to Texas. Not without her.

"Nancy, I've got this under control. You can take off."

She looked like she wanted to protest, but he sent her the steely gaze he'd perfected and used when new medics tried to flex their muscles and buck their training.

"Fine. But call me later and we can talk next steps."

He'd be calling her later—but not to chat. He needed to do this on his own.

"I'll… I'll walk you out, Nancy," Kelsey said. "Let's give them some time to get to know each other."

She sent Emma a longing look that cracked his chest open. There was so little he knew about

Kelsey—mostly just her charity work and job stuff from Page, while they were still working on saving their marriage. But Kelsey loved Emma. Whether or not that would work in his favor remained to be seen.

The women left and Liam allowed himself to exhale and look at his child. He traced her small, furrowed brows until they softened and she giggled—the best sound he'd ever heard. Her pale, amber-colored eyes—Page's eyes—were filled with joy.

"I'll make sure they stay that way," he whispered, breathing in her sweet scent. "Whatever it takes."

Emma threw herself against his chest as if she'd understood his promise. He flinched, then cradled her head, petrified he'd done something wrong when she wouldn't stop squirming.

"What's wrong, baby girl?"

Emma writhed in his arms, but it wasn't like she could tell him what he'd done.

"You're okay. Just support her back," Kelsey said, walking back in the room. "Her neck is strong enough to support her head now."

*Of course.* As soon as he moved his hand to her back Emma settled against him. *I should have known that.*

But he specialized in trauma—what did he know about caring for a child who couldn't even tell him what she needed?

"Thanks. I've got a lot to learn."

"You do. A book would help, but I guess…" She paused and he saw the war on her face. "I can answer any questions you have. She's a pretty easy baby."

It was clear she wanted to do what was best for Emma, but not if it meant losing her. He understood that feeling on a visceral level. So why did it surprise him to see it in her?

"I got a book…but it was about newborns. I don't think a single page of it applies now that I'm here, holding her."

It was a gift he didn't take for granted. So many things in the past year of his life could have gone a hair's width the other way and he'd have never met his daughter. The capture, the escape, the therapy he'd undergone to get things right…

"Hmm."

Her gaze settled on Emma, then drifted to him. He had the urge to squirm like Emma under Kelsey's watchful eye.

"Well, you're getting it. I wouldn't worry about it too much."

"Thanks. It's the most important thing to me… making sure I do this right."

"Me, too."

A tense silence settled between them. Their shared goal was also a conflicting one. Where one of them gained ground, the other lost it.

But it wasn't about them, was it? It was about Emma. Just like he and Page had agreed when she'd discovered the result of their attempted reconciliation.

A whisper of an idea took shape in his head. It would give him what he wanted most, while making sure he didn't do exactly what his own father had done—throw money at a nanny to raise his kid so he could build an empire.

"Anyway, you wanted to talk?" she asked.

"Yeah."

He thought through the two sudden shifts in his life, both happening within the past ten minutes.

"I can't live without Emma," he said, giving voice to the first.

Kelsey's face fell, but she remained stoic otherwise.

"What are you saying?" she asked.

"I also can't yank her away from the only life she's known with you."

Kelsey's arms folded over her chest.

"What are you saying?" she asked again.

Her eyes were wide and she took her bottom lip between her teeth. He recognized the hope in her gaze.

"I'm saying I want to find a way to stay here in L.A. so I can get to know Emma."

"You're *staying*?"

"I think so. I want as much time with this girl as I can get, but I don't think I can do it alone."

"I can."

*Wait. What?*

"You thought I'd just leave her here with you?" he asked.

A laugh bubbled up in his chest, even though this was the furthest thing from funny.

"What were *you* thinking?" she asked. "That you'd schlep her across the world with you when you deployed? I've been a single mom for half a year now, and I think I've done a pretty bang-up job."

Doubt crept along his skin. He hadn't expected a fight. Or for her to be right. She'd done a damn good job raising his child alone.

He shook his head.

"Let's start over. Kelsey. I've retired from the Army and I have a job lined up with Everson Health when I get back to Austin. But I think we can do this together—help each other to raise Emma. I'd like to do this together. But if you don't agree, I can take her back with me and figure it out from there."

"No. Please don't do that."

The crack in her voice was the first fissure in her reproving demeanor, the first glimpse of a real person behind her stony exterior.

"Please don't take her away."

"Okay. Then what do you say, Dr. Gaines? You in?"

# CHAPTER THREE

KELSEY CHEWED ON the end of her fingernail. Her manicure was shot to heck. Sort of like her nerves at the moment. Liam stuck his tongue out at Emma, who copied him, sticking hers out before giggling.

"She's going to keep that up at daycare now. Thanks."

"It's adorable," he said. "Plus, it's not like she's five and being rude to a teacher."

"That's your benchmark?" she asked Liam, who looked up, a quirky half-smile on his lips.

"I'm sorry. It's just… I didn't think she'd be able to do any of this," he said. "She's so smart."

"She is. Some of the other kids in her room at daycare aren't even crawling yet."

"Emma's crawling?"

Kelsey smiled in spite of herself. "Yep."

Liam's face beamed with pride.

"Thank you, Kelsey. I know this is unexpected, but you can see why I can't just tuck tail and leave my daughter behind, can't you?"

She paused, trying to find a way to be diplomatic. "I can. I guess I just figured when your dad—"

"I'm not my father," he said. It wasn't snippy, but firm. "Regardless of Page's feelings on my shortcomings as a husband, even she agreed on that point."

"Sorry. But I'm going to need you to explain, please. Because I'm not sure what it is you're asking for."

She kept her gaze pinned to his face, so the image of Emma curled against his strong chest didn't rattle her any more than she already was. Which was a mistake, since his cheeks were still damp with emotion and the smile he shot her was handsome enough to render her speechless.

*You'd better not*, her heart warned. *Liam isn't the enemy, but he's off-limits. Just minutes ago he was ready to take his child back to Texas and leave you in the dust.*

She might be in limbo about a million other things, but of both those facts she was certain.

"I'd like to stay in L.A. Get to know Emma—on a schedule that you're okay with, of course."

"What would Nancy say to that?"

Liam shook his head. "Don't care. I'm about to email that her services are no longer required."

"Why did you bring her at all?"

"My boss suggested that if I wanted to fight for custody, Nancy would be just the sort of person to get the job done...efficiently."

"But that's not what you want? Custody of Emma?"

"Not fully. Not yet. I'd like to try co-parenting with you first."

"What about the job in Texas? Right now it

seems like our goals are mutually opposed. I'm here, and you want to be there."

Liam didn't answer immediately, and in the space his pause created her breathing slowed. So much hinged on this man's sudden and explosive presence in her life. On one hand he was a stranger, bent on ripping her from the thing she loved most. On the other he was her late friend's husband, desperate for time with his daughter.

"You have a lot of questions."

"Shouldn't I?" she asked, frowning when a wicked grin spread on his face. "This is Emma's future we're talking about. Questions lead to answers that will change the course of her life. And both of ours, too."

"I agree. And I'd like to talk about spending some time in Texas with Emma at some point. But the bottom line is, I can't imagine figuring this out on my own. That's where you come in."

He gestured between himself and Kelsey and she swallowed hard.

"So, what's your plan?"

He chuckled, but it didn't have a hint of humor in it. "I don't have a damn clue. I'm making this up as I go."

He looked at the sleeping child in his arms and his cheeks flushed a color red that Kelsey hadn't seen on a man.

"Sorry. I don't have a *darn* clue. I guess the military still has a hold on me. I'll work on it, though."

"Thanks." That he cared enough to try and change his vocabulary sent a shot of awareness through Kelsey's heart. "She's too young to pick it up now, but that'll change soon. Maybe in a month or two."

"Yeah? That soon, huh? I guess I should look at getting a book about older babies so I know what I'm doing," he admitted.

As if Emma had just come to the same conclusion, she wriggled in his arms.

"Can I offer a suggestion?" Kelsey asked, her arms outstretched.

Liam hesitated, but then he nodded. "Sure," he said.

"Loosen your limbs and relax. You're not going to break her and she can feel your tension."

"She can?" He looked down, as if seeing his daughter for the first time. "How 'bout that, Emma-Bear?" he cooed.

Kelsey bristled at hearing the nickname.

"It's Emma-Bean."

"Maybe to you. I like Emma-Bear, and there's no reason we can't use both."

"She might get confused."

His smile was positively disarming. "Weren't you just saying she's incredibly smart?"

She grimaced, but relented. Still, her heart palpitated with this small shift in control. How much would change if she agreed to co-parent with Liam? How much would she have to give up?

Emma relaxed and nestled her head in the crook of his arm, dozing off in a matter of moments. Maybe it wouldn't be all bad…

"Would you like to head downstairs so we can talk about this?"

"Yeah. Sounds good. But can I…uh…can I walk with her? Without waking her up?"

Kelsey smiled. "You can."

No, he wasn't the enemy. A confused new father? Yes, definitely. A barrier to her guardianship over Emma? Maybe. Probably. But someone she should fear? She didn't think so.

The tension in her own shoulders released.

The three of them sat on her back patio, on furniture Kelsey hadn't ever used.

Emma snored softly against Liam's chest, and an umbrella shaded them. He smoothed Emma's hair and kissed her softly. Something primal tugged at Kelsey's heart, making it ache.

"So…logistics. You're thinking you'll move here? Does that mean working here too?"

He shrugged, his strong shoulders on display. Despite his being off-limits, Kelsey had noticed Liam's physicality in a way she hadn't expected. There were lots of beautiful men in Hollywood, but none who looked like their muscles had been earned outside of a gym. None that made her wonder if she'd ever open herself up to that kind of love again.

"I guess so. But it's expensive here—I know that

much. And I'd like to make my own way...not ask my family for help, if you know what I mean."

She did. Since her mom had died giving birth to Kelsey, and her dad had been in the Marine's, she'd been more or less making her own way her whole life.

"And you're a doctor?"

"Trauma surgeon. Combat trained but board certified. Why? Are you saying you'll help?"

Was she? Because if she agreed there was no going back.

"I need to know one thing first."

"Shoot," he said, his smile turning into a half-grin that was wholly distracting.

A tug of awareness pulled in the pit of her stomach.

*Oh, Page. I get what you saw in the guy.*

Thinking of her best friend was another reminder that she had no business being attracted to Liam. None whatsoever.

"Promise me you won't take her. Not without talking to me first."

Liam's smile fell, his eyes darting to hers as if he was trying to read her mind.

"I promise. If we think this co-parenting thing isn't working, we can come up with something that'll work for both of us."

"Why would you do that? I'm not her biological mom. I'm not even her adopted parent yet."

*Stop trying to talk him into taking your daughter.*

But she had to know his plans so she could build a defense around them.

"Because Page trusted you. And whether or not she and I were doing well, I trusted her judgment without question. Besides, I see how you are with Emma. I'd be a fool not to notice you're making her life better in every way possible."

Kelsey thought about that. And about what she stood to lose if she didn't take this deal of sorts.

But one thing still chipped away at Kelsey's resolve—something Liam had said about trusting Page. What would Page think now that Liam was home safe? Would she want him to be Emma's only guardian or would she stand by her letter to Kelsey? Was this agreement a middle ground, or a settling for all three of them?

For all she knew none of this would matter in a few months. The man might take a handful of three a.m. feedings, and half that in explosive diapers, and run back to Texas alone. Only time would tell, she supposed.

Kelsey had faith that things would shake out either way, although a tiny knot in her stomach twisted when she considered what it might cost her to have something so precious, only to lose it in the end.

But what choice did she really have?

"Okay," she said. "Let's figure this out together."

# CHAPTER FOUR

LIAM'S KNUCKLES ACHED from slugging the heavy bag at the hotel gym, and the skin on one had cracked open. Luckily his hands were mostly calluses anyway, so only a thin thread of blood rose to the surface.

He looked at his watch, twisted it so he could see through the long crack in the glass. The scar on the surface was a souvenir from his most recent deployment. It was quarter to noon. Time to meet up with Kelsey to figure out how to work out what he was calling the world's weirdest custody agreement.

No lawyers, no court, and only one biological parent. But two people committed to giving Emma the best life imaginable.

They could have worse odds on their side.

But the strangeness of the custody agreement wasn't the thing that sent him back to the bag for another punishing round of jabs and crosses. It was the look in Kelsey's eyes when she'd begged him not to take Emma away from her. Her hurt and pain had reached in and grabbed a part of his heart he'd assumed had been closed off after he'd split from Page. Hell, long before that if he was being honest.

And the oddest part? He'd had the urge to take that pain and hurt away.

*Not your job, Cap.*

No, it wasn't. And it would serve him well to remember that, since number one on his "Don't Become your Father" checklist was taking care of his daughter. Maybe twenty down there was something about being a good spouse, but nowhere did it say *Find the custodial parent of your daughter attractive.*

That was on the *other* list—the one he avoided at all costs.

Still, it had been two days since he'd seen the woman—and his daughter—and he was crawling out of his skin, counting down the minutes till they all met up again.

An hour and one very cold shower later, he had some clarity as he pulled up to her house and rang the bell. He was just concerned for someone who had influence over his daughter. And as for the countdown to see them… He was conflating his feelings about Kelsey with those for Emma. It wasn't anything more than that.

Not two seconds later Kelsey opened the door, sending Liam staggering backwards, almost toppling down the steps. He recovered his balance, but not his equilibrium, because…

*Damn.*

What was the word he'd used to describe her a few days ago? Severe? And what had he told himself about his feelings?

Yeah, that was all blown to hell.

She wasn't wearing as much make-up—just a

hint of mascara if he was noticing right. He only figured that much because the thin line of black around her eyes made them appear to be jade jewels set in stone. But it was more than her change in make-up that made him do a double take.

Replacing the dark, professional suit was a tan pencil skirt and button-down white blouse, both of which hugged curves he hadn't noticed before and would do well to forget about now, since his throat had gone conspicuously dry at the sight of her hips, one delicate yet strong hand on each as she appraised him.

She tossed her loose hair from over her shoulders, the light brown strands reflecting the sun, making it seem like it glowed from within.

Severe and untouchable?

*Nah, she was sex in a suit.*

A stirring in his stomach that had nothing to do with nerves replaced his earlier frustration. Leave it to his year-and-a-half-long drought to wake up his libido at the most inconvenient time imaginable.

"Hey, Liam. Come on in."

"Sure," he managed.

When was the last time he'd been rendered speechless? He couldn't recall.

"Uh…thanks for doing this. It means a lot that you're willing to help."

"No problem. Anything for Emma, right?"

"Exactly."

Mentioning his daughter—their daughter—

brought him back to the present, to Kelsey's role in his life. She was a co-parent. Nothing more.

"You know, I can suture that if you'd like." She indicated the bead of blood on his hand from the split skin.

"Not necessary. Just dry skin. And I'm just as capable of sewing up a superficial wound even if it wasn't."

"Sorry. I didn't mean you weren't—just that I can lend a hand if you need one. Can I at least get you a bandage?"

He sighed. *Not a good start.*

"Sure. And sorry. I'm just not used to having people care about my health. It's usually the other way around."

"I get it. I'm the same."

*Was she?* He ignored his visceral response to that information.

"We're out back. I'll grab the bandage and meet you out there."

*We?* But he didn't have time to ask.

She veered off towards where he assumed a bathroom would be, and he took his time considering her taste. It was modern, expensive, and, yes, somewhat cool, but exquisite. Something his mother might have appreciated.

A piece of art stretched on a canvas at least as tall as him adorned the wall to his left, three of the same to his right. Above him, the chandelier twinkled expensive light over the art, giving each piece an ethereal glow. He'd give her one thing—she knew how to put her money to use.

Kind of like his father in that way.

"You must be Captain Everson," a thick, rough voice said behind him.

It was the voice of a man who worked for a living, and when Liam turned around the stature of the man confirmed it. He was only an inch shorter than Liam's six-foot-four frame, but stockier. Muscles built from hard manual labor filled a flannel chambray shirt.

"Call me Liam. You must be Kelsey's father. A fellow vet, right?"

The green eyes appraising him were a lighter shade than the good doctor's, but they held the same intensity.

"Yes, on both accounts. Mike Gaines, former Marine—but don't hold it against me."

Liam smiled. He liked this guy, but could picture him at the Austin ranch house he'd grown up in more than in a home like this, in a city like L.A.

"Nice place your daughter has here," he said.

"It is. Suits her. I'd go nuts if I had to stare at this much white, but the backyard's something else. Care to see?"

Liam nodded, even though he'd been there only two days prior. "Lead the way."

"I wanted to tell you before my daughter joins us how sorry I am for your loss. It feels like a piece of yourself was cut off and you keep trying to use it, am I right?"

Liam nodded, his throat tight and hot all of a sudden. "It is. Your wife, too?"

It took a widower to know one, Liam thought, and even though he was new to the job, he recognized it now…the tough edge of loss in the man's smile that didn't reach his eyes.

"In childbirth, too. We had two healthy girls in our time together, though, so I still consider myself lucky."

"Mmm-hmm."

Liam gazed up at the doorframe as he passed through it to the balcony, hoping the heat behind his eyes would dissipate. He and Page had been on the cusp of divorce, but not because he hadn't cared about her. They just hadn't been a good fit.

"Here ya go. I figure you'd rather talk to this little one than me, so I'll get outta your hair. Make yourself at home."

Mike bent to retrieve a wide-eyed Emma from the Pack 'n Play and handed her to Liam. Like the first time he'd met his daughter, just days ago, he felt the tears fall and was powerless to stop them.

"Hey, Captain?"

Liam looked up at Mr. Gaines, wishing he could stop blubbering like a fool every time he was around this family. Emma placed her chubby little hands on his cheeks and tickled his lips with her finger. He laughed through his tears.

"Uh-huh?"

"I just wanted to add how grateful I am for your service. It's a heckuva place to be…where you're at right now."

"Thank you, sir."

"Call me Mike. She's pretty great, isn't she?" Mike asked, and then left the two of them alone on the deck.

Liam nodded, and Emma used what little strength she had at only half a year old to pull his face back to hers. Her forehead touched his and like a bolt of lightning Liam understood Mike's comment. This new life staring up at him through amber eyes consumed him.

*Did my dad ever feel like this about me? Or was he always distant?*

He considered both possibilities until Kelsey strode across the stone balcony. Then Liam's heart rate spiked.

"She looks like you," Kelsey said, placing a bandage and a tall glass of water in front of him.

Good timing, since hearing the sultry lilt of the way she ended each sentence on an exhale left his throat dry.

"You think so?"

"I do. Emma has the same tilt of her head that Page had, but she's clearly your daughter."

"You and Page spent a lot of time together?"

"Yeah, she lived in the guest bedroom half the time."

"She lived here? Like, in this house?"

He wouldn't have known, since he'd been deployed or in training workups eleven months each year. In fact, the sheer number of things he didn't know about his wife's life at the end of it ate at him. The high-risk aspect of her pregnancy…where she'd lived…the choice she'd made in Emma's guardianship. She might as well have been a stranger.

"On and off. Until she found out about Emma, after her last trip to Austin."

"When we agreed to make our split permanent?"

Kelsey nodded. "She wanted her own place then. Something she could make her own when she had custody of your child. I think before that she'd always held out hope it would work out between you two."

"I never got to see that. Her place. Her sister handled the estate, I think."

"It was cute, but nothing special. She didn't have anything in it yet. Then there was the complication and…"

"She never moved in."

"No."

His arms tensed and Emma must have sensed it, because she let out a small cry. Like defib paddles to his chest, the soft sound brought him back and he relaxed. There had been a time when he'd thought Page had thought him special, too, but that was a lifetime ago. Before their fights had spotlighted the infinite ways his past made him feel like he'd never be enough. Before Emma, or even the possibility of her, had brought him out of that way of thinking. Too late, but enough all the same.

Emma was wiggling out of his arms towards Kelsey, so he finally handed her over. His arms were grateful for the break, but his heart missed her instantly. It was always going to be this difficult, wasn't it? Giving her up at the end of a weekend or whatever arrangement they came to?

But she'd get the best of two worlds. A simpler, sparser one with him, while he fumbled through learning to be a dad, and a lavish, rich one with Kelsey, who knew what she was doing. He'd just have to learn to live with the ache when she wasn't around. Wasn't that what all parents did?

"Anyway, let's try to map this out," Kelsey said, interrupting his thoughts.

One leg was crossed over the other, showing off toned, tanned thighs. He kept his gaze on her eyes. She procured a pen and pad from behind her on the chair, somehow managing both with the sleeping infant in her arms. She nibbled on the end of the pen and he swallowed his feelings before they grew too big to contain.

"You're really going to stick around?" she asked.

"I want to. I'm not crazy about the upscale L.A. life, but I'm sure from what I've read people could use a trauma surgeon downtown."

"What about co-parenting? You're sure about this agreement?"

Liam let his gaze flicker over the slit in her skirt. "I am. Page told me enough about you to make me feel comfortable. This isn't a situation anyone wanted, but I'm committed to making it work. If it doesn't… Well, like I said, we can work out a custody plan then."

"You're not what I expected."

Her lips twisted into something resembling a smile. It was kind of cute…the way her eyes crinkled around the edges.

He chuckled. "I'm sure I'm not. I can only imagine what Page said about me… And the crummy thing is, most of it was probably true back then."

"She told me you two struggled, that she wanted more. But she…she cared about you—even after she knew you were over."

"Hmm… She didn't have to be that kind. But I've done enough work on myself that I don't recognize that guy anymore."

She seemed to consider that.

"Okay, then… I'm assuming you haven't found a place yet, right?"

"Nope. That's phase two—after a job. But I'm not sure I can stay locally. I've only got military retirement pay, but I'd like to avoid asking my dad to help out financially. So that would mean a commute for when we trade Emma, but I'm sure we can figure out someplace to meet up."

Kelsey put the pen on the pad of paper and

leaned forward, still somehow avoiding waking the languid infant draped across her arms.

"Why don't you stay here?"

He hoped the look he shot her—confusion mixed with something less inhibited—implied that it wasn't a good idea. And if he was an artist, he'd commission a whole piece in the shade of red her cheeks turned as she realized how her question had come across.

"I mean in the cabin I have on the property. It's not being used, and you can make it your home as long as you need."

"Why would you offer that to a stranger?"

"You aren't a stranger; you're Emma's dad. And you're trusting me to help raise her. For now," she added when he opened his mouth to reply. "And if I'm being honest, it serves my designs, too. I don't know how to be away from her for very long, and if you're here I won't have to. And if you ever need help with her, I'll be next door."

He considered that. It checked a lot of boxes. It would probably be cheaper than any of the dumps he'd find in town. He knew the landlady already—and trusted her. But the stone tipping the scales was that he'd never be far from Emma either.

"I'll insist on paying rent."

"Fine. If that's what you need. It's furnished, but you can make it your own."

"And, to be honest, I'm not sure I'll be comfortable taking her overnight—not until we find our rhythm, anyway."

"That's fine. Just let me know when you're ready."

Liam sipped at his water, looking out over the expansive deck to the ocean below. It was more than he deserved.

"Thank you. I've put the end of my marriage behind me, but I know I've still got work to do to build your trust—and Emma's, too. I don't take that lightly."

"Good. Me neither. Now, let's talk about getting you a job. Are you set on downtown?"

Liam smiled so hard he felt it in his cheeks. He hadn't been sure at all about coming out here, about meeting Emma and what would come of that first meeting, but now, deep in his soul—the one he'd built from scratch after the first one had been obliterated in combat—he rejoiced.

Things were shaping up for the better for the first time in his life, and he had a feeling he owed a lot of it to the beautiful woman holding his child.

But imagining her as more than that was as off-the-table as imagining how he was going tell his dad to find someone else to fill the Everson Health board seat. Because Liam wasn't going home anytime soon.

# CHAPTER FIVE

KELSEY STRIPPED OFF the latex gloves and smiled down at her patient, a twenty-seven-year-old socialite, eight months along in her first pregnancy. The woman's cheeks glowed from within and a gentle peace shone through her smile as she toyed with her wedding ring. Even now, just shy of a thousand deliveries into her career, Kelsey still marveled at the majestic beauty of a woman in love and about to give birth.

A small thread tugged at Kelsey's heart, in the space she'd never been able to fill. She loved Emma fiercely, but the child drove home the point Mike had been quick to see: Kelsey wanted a family. A *complete* family. Kelsey craved falling into the arms of a man who adored her and shared her plans and dreams. Dex hadn't been willing to entertain the idea of marriage—not being as married to his work as he was. When he'd left because of Emma it had hurt, but mostly because it had shattered the image of a complete family she'd curated.

She swallowed back a defeated sigh. Even without Dex in the picture anymore, that idyllic image probably wasn't in her cards. Moments like this—helping a patient through the trying but beautiful process of carrying a life within her—were enough. They had to be.

And yet none of it—the longing or the work—

was enough to distract her from her father's texts about Liam's removals truck arriving.

*I'm proud of you, hun. Offering the cabin to him is a move in the right direction for all of you. Emma most importantly. You should feel good about this.*

That would be nice, but all Kelsey had felt since she'd introduced Liam to Kris Offerman, the Chief Medical Officer at Mercy Hospital, was fear. Fear over losing Emma…over not knowing how Liam was raising her when Kelsey wasn't around. Inherently, she knew he'd never hurt Emma. But look what had happened when she'd given up control with Page and let someone else into her carefully designed world of rules and procedures.

The worst fear was knowing she couldn't stop any of this from happening. At most, Emma was only half her responsibility now, and even helping Liam with a job and a home nearby wouldn't guarantee he'd raise their daughter the way she would.

She addressed her patient. "You're only a couple weeks away from meeting… Mason, is it?"

Her patient, Maggie, grinned and laughed. "It is. I finally won that one. We settled on Christopher for the middle name, to honor Jeff's father. I said he gets to pick for the second kid. If it's a girl, though, I'm taking that back."

Kelsey laughed, too. "Oh, yeah? What name do you have picked out for a little girl?"

"I was thinking of Paige. With an 'i.'"

Kelsey wiped the rest of the gel off Maggie's stomach and tried to keep the smile on her face. *Page.* A name that would haunt her forever. She couldn't say as much to Liam, nor to her father—not when they'd both endured so much more loss—but she missed her friend.

"That's a lovely name," she managed.

"Thanks. Hey, how is your daughter? You said on my last visit you had a six-month-old, right?"

Kelsey blinked back a tear.

*For now.*

"That's true."

"Aw… Do you have any photos? I'd love to see her."

Kelsey got out her phone, but as soon as she had her photos pulled up her cell chimed with the ringtone she'd attached to her boss—the *Yellowstone* theme song. The woman was all Beth Dutton, which Kelsey wished she could channel right about now. That woman didn't give up an ounce of herself for anyone else.

*Except the handsome rancher.*

Kelsey ignored the image of Liam that popped into her head at that particular moment.

"Can you excuse me for a second? I have to take this."

"Of course. It's good to see you again, Dr.

Gaines. Next time we see each other you'll be delivering my first baby."

"Looking forward to it. Tell your husband I'm thrilled about his Emmy nomination, okay?"

Kelsey swiped open the call as she walked out. "Hey, Kris."

"Can I see you in my office when you have a sec?"

Leave it to Mercy's CMO to cut the pleasantries and get right to business. Kelsey liked having privileges at a hospital with a competent woman like Kris at the helm.

"Sure. I have some time now."

"Perfect. See you soon."

Kris hung up, leaving Kelsey feeling worried.

Kelsey had taken some personal leave to help Liam clean out the cabin and make room for his furniture, but that was up. Dropping Emma at daycare had been near impossible that morning, because she'd heard whispers there that Dex was back from his four-months away, representing Mercy Hospital at an international mental health summit in Africa. She hadn't seen him since he'd unceremoniously walked out of her house and her life the day she'd agreed to be Emma's guardian.

Was that what this impromptu meeting was about? Whether she could work around the hospital's Chief of Psychiatry, who'd dumped her for doing the right thing?

Because she could. She was a professional, even if her insides argued otherwise.

Yeah, today was going to Hades in a handbasket pretty quick. If Barb hadn't kicked her out of the daycare room after she'd dropped Emma off, she wouldn't have come in at all. Being away from the baby made her skin itch, her breath hard to pull into her lungs. At least she could stop by and steal a kiss or two during her lunch break later.

She got to Dr. Offerman's office in less than two minutes, successfully avoiding Dex in the hallways. After knocking and being told to enter, Kelsey went in, guns blazing.

"Hey, Kris. I just want to say, yes, I know he's back, and, no, it won't be a problem. We parted on good terms and I've moved on."

She plastered a smile on her face that probably looked like it was sewn on. But it fell when Kris sent back a smirk very much akin to a certain Dutton woman.

"I'm so glad to hear that, but I didn't doubt your professionalism for a moment. Which is why I'm asking you to take Dr. Liam Everson on a tour of the building, since you recommended him for a position."

As Kelsey took stock of the room she realized Liam was there, staring at her with a similar mischievous grin.

"I wouldn't say I *recommended* him so much as—"

"It's a good fit—don't worry. We were just catching up about his late wife's work with your Foundation and he volunteered to pick up some of those duties once he settles in."

"What?" Kelsey asked, her voice shrill.

*So much for professional.*

"Oh, that's not necessary,' she went on. 'We've filled her vacant spot already. Owen will take up donations going forward. Thanks, though."

She worked up a smile for Liam, who was probably just being nice, but she had to draw a line somewhere.

She'd built the Foundation from scratch and she ran it the way she wanted to, to serve the dozens of women in need of her care. Kelsey needed something that was just hers. Something he couldn't take out of her hands.

"If you change your mind, you know where to find me. Anyway, I was just filling Dr. Offerman in on our rather unconventional arrangement," he said.

*Unconventional.*

That was one way of thinking about it. Twice already she'd stopped herself from ogling him as he ran the trails in front of the main house. And seeing his truck pull into the hospital today had sent her heart almost tachycardic.

"Yes, it is. But…uh…we're making it work."

"Great to hear. We're glad to have you on board, Liam. Oh, and Kelsey?" Kelsey turned back. "*He* doesn't come back until tomorrow."

Kelsey nodded. She'd forgotten she'd aired her dirty relationship laundry to the man she shared this "unconventional arrangement" with. *Oh, let the earth swallow her whole.*

When Kris's door closed behind them, Kelsey felt Liam's eyes on her.

"Old boyfriend?"

"Oof… We're not gonna let that slide, huh?" She smiled weakly, hoping for some hint of mercy.

"Nope. My past is out there on the public news for everyone to pick apart. I hope you can trust me enough to share a little of yours. Since…you know…we're raising a daughter together."

When had they crossed the border from passably respectful to…friendly? He winked at her and there went her pulse again. He was going to be responsible for giving her an arrhythmia.

"You make a good point." Even if he'd bordered on the edge of flirting to make it. "What do you want to know?"

"What happened?" he asked, his face growing serious again.

"Well, we broke up five months ago and I haven't seen him since. Since he's now back from a four-month health summit, and is Chief of Psychiatry here at Mercy, that's probably going to change."

"Why did you leave him?"

"Why do you assume I'm the one who left?"

He shoved his hands in his pockets and shrugged. "I just can't imagine why he'd want to let you go."

"Pshh! That's a laugh." Her cheeks flashed with heat at the unexpected compliment, though.

"No, it's not. You're smart—obviously."

"I'll tell my dad you said so."

He dipped his chin. "Please do. But, jokes aside, you care more than anyone I've ever met."

Good grief, was her body always going to betray her by flushing her skin and kickstarting her poor heart when he said things like that?

"Well, thank you. It's nice of you to say. But actually, he's the one who left me. Turns out he didn't really want a family and 'all that nonsense.' He'd always said as much, but I guess I was always hoping…"

"That he'd change for you?"

"Something like that."

"In my experience, people don't change for anyone other than themselves."

"I know. But that doesn't mean it didn't sting when I told him I wanted to adopt Emma."

"*That's* why he left?" he asked. "Because you did the right thing?"

She smiled inwardly at the incredulity in his voice. "Yep. But it's fine."

"Yeah, I don't think I want to meet the guy. I'm a little worried my military training will trump the part of me that wants to do no harm."

"Really, it's fine. We're better off the way we are now, anyway." She realized how her words could be construed and changed tactics. "How about you? Was it Page you were waiting on to change? She never said as much, but I always…wondered, I guess."

"No, it was me and my warped thoughts about my own worth. Honestly, if I was waiting for anything, it was for her to realize I wasn't able to give her the life she wanted. But she stuck around and supported me anyway."

He gazed down the hall at something Kelsey couldn't see.

"So, I threw myself into work and she finally decided to move on. I'll never regret her coming back one more time to try and fix me—fix *us*—but I wish she'd had a chance to be happy without me, you know?"

Kelsey walked on down the hall, thinking about that.

"I hear what you're saying, but wait…"

She put out a hand. That it landed on Liam's forearm—his very *strong* forearm—wasn't intended. Still, heat raced up her arm from the spot where her flesh rested on his.

Liam stopped beside her, his gaze pinned to where her hand rested.

"Sorry," she said, dropping her hand. "But you did."

"I did what?"

"Change. For Emma. And you made Page happy in the end. She was thrilled you both wanted Emma and that you might be able to co-parent."

"You're right. I did. For Emma, partly, but also because I'd never forgive myself if I let her feel one ounce of what I did growing up."

"What was that like?"

She met Liam's gaze, saw the flecks of gold around his eyes glittering with hurt.

"Nothing, really. It was like living alone without anyone to bounce ideas off or tell you they were proud of you. No one to make you meals or cuddle up and read a book with you at the end of the day. My dad's only child was the hospital. It almost turned me off medicine altogether, but I couldn't let him take that from me, too."

"I'm sorry, Liam."

He sighed and tried for a smile, but it didn't reach his eyes. God, what she wouldn't do to take that pain from him. He'd endured so much.

"Me too. Wow. We're a pair of sad sacks, aren't we? Emma's really won the lottery with our pathetic backstories to support her childhood."

Kelsey laughed. "She'll be resilient, that's for sure."

"Anyway, thanks for this. I'm grateful for the tour. And everything else."

"Um…good. I mean, you're welcome." She cleared her throat. "Do you want to see where Emma gets to hang out when my dad is busy?"

"She's here?"

Kelsey nodded.

"Then, yeah, of course."

They kept walking until they turned a corner and landed in front of Mercy's daycare facility. His eyes went wide and his brows crashed together when he saw the three rooms, all brightly lit, with murals boasting scenes from favorite children's books on each wall and toys for every age on shelves the kids could reach. Kelsey knew they were lucky to have such a fun, safe haven for Emma when she couldn't be with family.

"It's incredible," he said. "She likes it?"

"Loves it. Loves the women, mostly. Especially Barb—the older woman in back there. Emma practically leaps out of my arms into hers."

While Liam put on the protective socks required to go into the play area, Kelsey added him to the approved pick-up and drop-off list. Her hands shook, but it was one of many concessions she'd have to make if they were going to raise Emma together. It was better than having her own name removed altogether.

"You three are a cute family," commented Jen, one of the new attendants.

"Oh, we're not—" Kelsey started.

"And, wow. He's good with her," Jen added. "You're so lucky."

The young woman gazed starry-eyed at Liam as he sat beside Emma and she giggled and clapped her hands. Liam laughed heartily.

Kelsey's chest tightened. He *was* incredible with Emma. Confusion swirled in her stomach.

On paper, a man like Liam was everything she was looking for—someone who wanted kids *and* a career of his own. A man who would love those kids fiercely. But even thinking about him in the abstract like that was a betrayal. He was Page's widower.

"We should get going," she called over to him.

His lips fell into a frown, but he got up, kissed the top of Emma's head and whispered something in her ear Kelsey couldn't hear.

"Thanks for bringing me. I like seeing her happy like that. God, it's crazy to think she'll get as big as some of those other kids in there, isn't it?"

"It is."

Her only hope was she'd be there to see it.

They walked down the hall to the next step on their tour—the ER.

"Ah, the smell of antiseptic. Gotta love the ER."

He smiled, but the grin fell when the ER doors hissed open to reveal paramedics rushing a gurney in. A patient lay on top, his chest covered in blood, but no wound was visible from their vantage point. He writhed in pain and his screams echoed across the ER.

"GSW!" the paramedic called out. "Seventeen years old, bradycardic and oxygen at eighty."

Kelsey glanced around. Two nurses ran out from behind the station and started taking down vitals, but there wasn't a doctor in sight. Before Kelsey could call someone to page one of the two trauma

docs they had on staff—Christensen and Piper—
Liam had shed his jacket and draped it over a chair.

"I need to jump in. Do you mind?"

"N-no, not at all—" she stammered, but he was
already diving in and helping the patient.

The juxtaposition between the man she watched
remove the patient's bloody shirt and the one who'd
just kissed his six-month-old was jarring.

"Was he ever unconscious?" he asked the paramedic, who shook his head.

"On and off in the rig, but not since we pulled
up."

"Any signs of a bullet?"

"No exit wound—likely still in there, tearing
stuff up."

"Thanks. You cauterize this?" Liam asked the
EMT, who nodded. "Good work. You saved his
life."

Liam turned to the nurses, who watched him
through wary eyes as they donned gloves. "I'm the
new trauma surgeon Dr. Offerman hired. Can I get
you two to assist?"

"Of course," one said, while the other just nodded blankly at actually being asked for anything.
Usually they got nothing but demands barked from
a grumpy doctor.

"Great—thanks. I need a liter of blood and three
more on hand. Get me a bed and a CT of his stomach. I need to find that bullet before it does any
more damage."

"Yes, Doctor," they said in unison.

Where Liam had been nervous with Emma, he was confident and calm in this environment. Kind, even. A natural. And Kelsey watched, awe mixing with respect in a dizzying combination that made her lightheaded.

*Funny that when he seems most in control and self-assured, I'm untethered. In other circumstances, we'd make a good team.*

"Is there a trauma room open?" Liam asked.

Kelsey pointed to the corner of the ER at an open trauma bay.

Liam continued to take charge while the nurses prepped IVs and a bed for the patient. "All right," he said. "Tina, could you call up to the OR and let them know we're coming? Susan, I need his labs yesterday—can you ask the lab tech to hand 'em over as soon as possible? Let's go, team."

Team? Since when?

*Since now, silly. Looks like you made a good call, getting him set up here.*

No one questioned Liam, or what he was doing. Kelsey wouldn't have either. He exuded the status of most qualified in the room, and as Kelsey watched him roll up his sleeves and shut the door to the trauma room she didn't have any doubt the patient was in good hands. This was Liam's church and the ER was his pulpit.

*Watch out*, her heart warned. *This one's special.*

* * *

The day passed slowly, and Kelsey's patients were a blur of faces and due dates behind the fog of wondering how Liam's patient was faring. She considered heading down to the ER and asking around, but thought better of it. The less she engaged with Liam, the better. Watching him at work, competent and confident, had unraveled something in her chest that she'd kept wound tight since Page died and Dex left.

What would happen if he kept tugging at that loose thread? What would he undo—and, more terrifying, what would that do to Kelsey?

She got home at five, excited at the prospect of seeing the one face that could wash the day's drama away in an instant, but found her house empty.

*What the...?*

Dad should be there with Emma.

Panic crept over her skin. She tore through the rooms until she heard a sound that hadn't rung through her hallways in months, maybe years.

*Laughter. From her father.*

And a high-pitched squeal she'd recognize anywhere.

*Emma.*

The joyous sounds came from the balcony, so she left her shoes by the door and ran outside.

No one was there, but a quick glance over the railing explained the situation. On the sandy half-moon-shaped bay that abutted her property, her dad, Emma, and *Liam* were playing at the edge of the surf. Every time a wave rolled in and tickled Emma's toes she squealed, until one of the men lifted her into the air. Then the squeals turned into cries of absolute glee.

A smile spread across Kelsey's face. This was what she'd hoped for most of her life—for her dad to have a reason to laugh again.

The whole scene repeated itself, but one wave was stronger than they all expected and the guys got splashed with chilly salt water. Kelsey surprised herself by giggling as well.

Curiosity about Liam's day at work combined with an urge to join in the fun.

"Hey, guys!" she called down.

Her dad looked up and waved at her, gesturing that she come and join them. She nodded and pointed to her pants and suit jacket, gesturing that she'd change first. When he raised his eyebrows at her and shrugged as if to say, *Why wait?* she laughed.

"What am I doing?" she asked herself as she shed her jacket and rolled up her pant legs.

But she couldn't take her eyes off her daughter's small hand in the very large, very tanned hand of Liam. And she really tried not to notice the sinewy forearms attached to that hand, or the strong, cut shoulders attached to those forearms.

Liam could model for military recruitment ads, or even underwear ads if he wanted to. Even if she wasn't allowed to consider him attractive personally, she knew he had a certain rugged appeal that would make most hot-blooded people take a second look.

She recalled what those hands had looked like as he'd worked to save his patient just hours before. They were capable of so much...

"Hey there, Bug. We found out this little miss likes the ocean as much as we do."

Liam dipped Emma's toes into the waves once more and she screeched with joy.

"I saw. It's adorable."

And gut-wrenching. They couldn't pretend to be one, big, happy family if Liam wasn't sure he'd stay in California.

"Hey, Kels." Liam grinned like he'd won the lottery, not spent all day in an L.A. emergency room.

"Hi, Liam. I hope your first day went smoothly after that first patient?"

"It did. The guy is doing great, and his family's pretty relieved. Wrong place, wrong time, but a mistake he'll recover from."

"I'm so glad to hear that. He looked rough, coming in."

Liam handed Emma to Mike and walked over to Kelsey. This close, she caught the scent of salty air mixed with something more masculine on Liam. Pine? Sandalwood? Her stomach flipped and, despite the moisture in the air, she had trouble swallowing.

"Thanks again for setting me up. I was worried I wouldn't fit in at Mercy, but it worked out okay."

"Why did you think you wouldn't fit in there?"

He gave one of his signature shrugs. "It's a pretty fancy hospital."

Kelsey opened her mouth to protest—Mercy wasn't *fancy* just because it valued its patients' experiences—but Liam kept going.

"I'm more used to shacks with unsterilized hot pokers than operating rooms with galleries. But I've got to say it felt so good being back under the OR lights with tools that work. It was a rush and… I dunno… Made me feel like myself again. The old me, who used to dream of helping people on that scale. Thank you for that."

*Dammit, Liam.*

Just when she'd thought she'd found a flaw in the guy, he had to go and say something incredible, putting her in her place. Which, of course, he'd bever actually do.

She smiled, even though she had to swallow a groan of frustration.

*Why did this man have to be so perfect?*

"So, how'd you end up down here?" she asked her dad, switching tack.

"It was Liam's idea, actually."

"Oh, yeah? It's a great day for it."

She bent down to kiss Emma's head and noticed a long scar along one of Liam's bare feet.

He'd been burned. Horrifically.

A shiver traced her spine. She kept forgetting what he'd overcome to be with his daughter.

"Sure is. I had Emma in the front pack, walking the gardens, and Liam was headed to the water for a swim. He invited us, and—well, we've been down here for an hour now. Emma cries every time we try to leave."

"Is that right, little miss?" Kelsey laughed. But worry stifled her joy. "An hour? Did you—?"

"Yes, we sunscreened her," Liam said, his eyes still pinned to Emma, who was splashing her feet in the shallow water.

But he caught Kelsey's gaze for just a moment, sending her a smile strong enough to weaken her knees.

"I read that you have to in the parenting book I just picked up."

He shot her a wink again, but her heart deflected that one.

"Thanks," Kelsey said.

A feeling of uselessness washed over her. Her hands hung limp at her sides, despite the weight lifted off them. The guys had it covered. It should have calmed her to see that Emma was safe with these two, but it only meant she wasn't needed. And if Liam ever saw it the same way…

She shuddered, and suppressed the fear that tried to creep in, too.

*He's not Dex. He won't leave; he promised.*

"By the way, Mike, you've got to teach me how

to do one of those wrap things," said Liam. "I can't figure out how to keep her from slipping right through."

"You bet. That'll be lesson number two."

"What was lesson number one?" Kelsey asked, grabbing a slice of the pizza one of them had brought down. The cheese and chewy crust were delicious.

"How to babyproof a sixty-year-old cabin," Liam said, laughing. "It's a work in progress."

"Well, I'm glad you're able to put that place to use. My father refused it, even though his place was only supposed to be a shed."

"Hey. Don't knock the shed. That cabin has too much space for my needs. Anyway, I'm gonna take Emma upstairs to get changed. Why don't you eat some more and enjoy the sun and come up when you're ready. No rush, Kels."

Her dad kissed her cheek and brought Emma close enough that Kelsey could kiss her daughter and tell her goodbye for now. She inhaled the infant's scent, marveling at how it stayed so particular to her, even if it had adopted the salt from the ocean and briny air.

When her dad walked Emma over to Liam, who brushed Emma's sparse tufts of hair back and looked into her eyes, Kelsey's heart fluttered. She remembered what she'd first thought when she'd met him.

*He isn't the enemy. He's lost so much in this, too.*

Liam was gazing out over the water, the light reflecting off it giving his skin an otherworldly glow. Like she needed any more visual ammunition to make her think about him as the handsome medical captain he was.

"She's incredible, isn't she? Like her own little person."

Kelsey smiled. Emma connected her to this man, for better or worse. And keeping Emma happy and healthy was their priority. Which meant she should let up a little about Liam's parenting choices; Emma was certainly thriving under his love.

"She's magnificent."

"She looks so much like Page... And that's great. I just wish there was some of me in there, too. You know?"

Kelsey nodded. "There is. She's stubborn, for one."

He chuckled, but his eyes were focused on something distant.

Her chest clenched. In her line of work loss was inevitable—expected to a certain degree. There was even a name for it: critical loss threshold. But hearing the name of the colleague who'd become her friend, remembering her quirks, facing her ex-husband, and her daughter's face that looked more and more like Page's every day... It was suffocating.

"Yeah, there's that," he said. "But what if she misses her mom, you know? How am I supposed to admit to my daughter when she's old enough that I left her mom behind, knowing full well she was pregnant?"

He turned back to look at her and it was as if the sunlight had trapped itself in his eyes. Gold emanated from their center. Her stomach did that strange little flip that biologically made no sense. She wasn't hungry, or nervous, but it wouldn't let up.

"I should have been there for Emma," he said. "No matter what was going on with Page and me. I never should have left on that tour."

He left it at that, so she did as well. She didn't need to know the man's innermost secrets for them to be good co-parents to Emma. And that was priority number one. If only her heart could ignore that tentative smile of his…

*Oh, boy.* This whole co-parenting with a surgeon-slash-handsome-war-hero thing was going to be harder than she thought.

# CHAPTER SIX

LIAM TOOK ONE of the trails by the house, curiosity winning over self-preservation. Maybe he'd just peek in to see if she was home. He could always use the sleeping infant on his chest as an excuse to drop by.

Oh, who was he kidding? He just wanted to see her again, period. Whether or not that was a good idea.

"What do you think, Emma? Should we check and see if Mom is home?"

He kissed the top of her head and a small sigh escaped her pursed lips.

Emma didn't answer, of course, but that didn't stop him from checking himself. *Mom?* When had he come to think of Kelsey as Emma's mother? It wasn't a bad development, just an interesting one, given the way he felt about the woman, not to mention the way his sadness about Page missing out on their daughter's life had begun to dissipate.

Whether *that* was a good or bad thing remained to be seen.

He'd meant what he'd told Kelsey about the hospital feeling like a good fit, and that being back in an OR had made things clearer for him. But what about what he didn't say?

Kelsey in a hot little pant suit, playing at the water's edge with her polished toes, the way the salt dried in cute white half-moons on her tanned skin—that had thrown the rest into a burn pile and lit the match.

All Liam wanted was a calm moment with his daughter—or a stiff drink to consider their future. But he couldn't get his mind off Kelsey. How she smiled and the sun seemed to shine just a little brighter. Or how when she came around he couldn't keep the smile from his own face.

*Ugh. I'm in trouble.*

Forget the drink. He needed to run out his frustration and, while he was at it, sprint out the image seared into the back of his lids of Kelsey's light brown waves blowing in the ocean breeze while she overlooked them from the balcony.

Damn if she wasn't driving him to distraction.

Halfway down the dirt trail that led from his cabin—or maybe mini-mansion would be a more apt description—he ran into Mike.

"Well, hey there. It looks like you got the hang of the wrap, huh?"

Mike tickled Emma's cheek but she didn't budge. Liam smiled. These moments were just normal, but he didn't think he'd ever tire of holding his daughter or chatting with Mike and Kelsey. They were like…well, like *family*—even if he still had to figure out what that meant.

"Sure did. Thanks for the lesson, Mike. You should run a blog for guys trying to figure out this whole parenting thing. You'd make a killing."

"Not sure what a blog is, but it sounds fishy. I'll stick to helping you when I can. Speaking of which, where are you two headed?"

"I was gonna see if Kelsey wouldn't mind some baby time so I could get in a quick run. Need to get some thoughts cleared up."

"She's out for one herself, but why don't I take the little miss? I've been itching to show her my new toolbox. She loves me slamming the top down on the old one and making a noise ."

Liam chucked. This man had a world to teach him about being a good dad—something he'd never get from his own father. The thirty-eight-year-old ache cracked open again.

"If you don't mind, that would be great."

Liam took Emma out of the wrap and held her while Mike worked at the intricate web of fabric. When Emma was safely swapped over, Liam stretched his hamstring, which was screaming at him for walking out of the door without loosening up first. Getting older wasn't for the faint of heart.

"You run, too?" he asked Mike.

"Nah. Not with these knees. Ruined by my own time in the Marines. But I get out and walk every morning. Keeps my head clear."

"You did a combat tour?"

"Two with the third division at the end of the war. Not quite special forces, but our company was special in its own right. First to shoot one of our own in the backside, so there's that." Mike chuckled.

"We had some men like that on my first push. Didn't make it far. Did you do twenty and retire?"

Mike shook his head. "Didn't get the chance. Ten years in I lost Ana, my wife. So I course-corrected and went into teaching at the local college. On the weekends I volunteer at the VA clinic with Kels. Help out wounded vets. It fills the days."

"Huh… That sounds familiar."

He'd forgotten Kelsey had lost her mother, too. And so young.

Liam raked his hands over his cheeks. The stubble scratched his palms. "How come Kelsey doesn't talk about her mom?"

"I suspect she's not over the guilt of it yet. I can't seem to convince her it's not her fault."

"Of course it wasn't. I mean, she was a newborn."

"Well, maybe you can make some headway there. She's been opening up more since you got here. Nightmares seem to be fading, too. I can't tell you how much I appreciate that."

"Thanks, Mike. Being here's helping me, too. More than I thought it would."

He made a note to ask Kelsey about these nightmares. He'd done some trauma work with vets to help them overcome PTSD-related night terrors.

"You doing okay with the rest of it, son?"

"The war or the job?"

"Losing your wife. Kelsey mentioned you weren't on the best of terms at the end, but that doesn't mean it won't leave a mark."

Liam looked down at Emma's flushed cheeks. He knew they got that way when she slept. He also knew her hair would stand up in the back when she woke up. He could picture the way her lips would curl into a yawn when she was waking—all because he was there, living alongside his daughter. Page didn't cross his mind so much now that Emma—and Kelsey—took up his thoughts.

"I'm good, actually. I did a ton of work on myself before I came out here, so that was behind me and I could show up for Emma. I'm not cured, or anything, but I've got some good tools in my own toolbox." He smiled. "Anyway, I'm mostly sad she didn't get to know this perfect angel, here."

"Hmm… I understand that more than most. She's got you to keep her mom's memory alive for her, though."

"Good point. And wishing it was different won't make it so. I can't make up an alternative future any more than I can change the weather. I think…" he hesitated, never having said what he was about to say out loud. "I think we can make the best of what we have."

"Well said, Liam. You're a good man—and a great dad."

Liam's throat swelled, making it hard to breathe.

He kicked at a clump of dirt at his feet. The sun was setting and a chill passed over his exposed skin.

"Thanks. And you should know Kelsey's a helluva doctor and an even better mother."

"It makes me happy to hear you say that. She may not share Emma's DNA, like you do, but that little girl has been the center of her world just the same."

Mike nodded before shoving his hands in his pockets, then set out in the way he'd been heading, Emma in tow.

"Hey, Mike? Thank you."

Mike stopped but didn't turn around. "You're welcome. Have a good run, Liam."

Liam smiled. He took off on his run, his energy renewed after what had to be the oddest, but most helpful five-minute talk he'd ever had.

An hour later, though, he hobbled back to the cabin hungry and barely able to put any pressure on his right leg.

At the door, he reached down to untie his muddy shoes and felt a snap in his hamstring.

"Damn it!" he cursed, sitting down in front of the door. He couldn't even bend his knee.

*Some special forces guy I'm shaping up to be. And a worse medic. Because I should know better.*

He wondered how long he'd be stuck sitting there as the minutes ticked by.

"What happened to you?"

The voice he'd spent eight miles trying to get out

of his head was back, with an undertone of concern that had an uncanny knack for tangling his insides since he'd first heard it two weeks ago.

*And of course I'm laid up, looking weak. Not the impression I wanted to give Kelsey.*

"Uh…nothing. Just stretching."

Liam looked up, the sweat from his hair and his forehead dripping into his eyes, blurring his vision. All he could make out was the figure he'd also tried to get out of his head, but with far less success.

He pressed the heels of his palms to his eyes and rubbed vigorously. When he opened his eyes again he tried to swallow, but between the run and the vision in front of him there wasn't any moisture to make that happen.

"Nice try, Captain. I heard you scream from my house. You okay?"

*Am I? Not exactly. For so many reasons.*

His lips twisted into a half-smile. "Nope. Not really."

"I guess, given the fact that I've promised to do no harm, you're gonna need my help," Kelsey said, smiling.

He shook his head, buying himself time to acclimate to Kelsey in a sports bra and tights, her hair pulled back in a tight ponytail. The off-white pant suit had been enough of a shock to his system, showing off curves he didn't want to think about too much. But this look… Well, if he'd been having trouble forgetting her before, it would be impossible now.

"I'm okay—really. I just pulled something. Feels like my femoris."

She bent down and stretched out his right leg, sending a shooting pain from his knee to his butt. So much for the relaxing run. He was tight as he'd ever been, and as for the spot where Kelsey's hand rested on his thigh... The skin beneath it burned like it'd been branded.

"What are you doing?" he asked, wincing as the muscle burned.

"I'm helping. Looks like your bicep femoris."

"Yeah. I said that."

It worked, though, because the burn faded to a dull ache.

"So," she said, gazing up at him with those green eyes he'd dreamed about these past few nights. "Did you warm up before taking off like a bat outta hell?"

"No," he admitted sheepishly.

"Well, there you go."

She shook her head at him, making him feel very much like a chastised kid. Again, not the impression he wanted to give her.

"Can you stand? Because I'd like to take a look at it."

"You don't have to—" he started, but she waved him off, tucking her arm under his and lifting.

She was stronger than she looked. And the thin

gleam of moisture on her skin glittered like diamonds when the sun hit it.

"Shh… It's my job. Just get inside and let me work my magic."

"You double as a PT in your free time?" he asked.

"Ha-ha. You're pretty smart there, soldier. I actually started physical therapy in my undergrad."

He hissed in a labored breath as she opened the door and guided him over the threshold. "What made you switch to obstetrics?" he asked.

"My mom, actually. When I did my third-year rotations through the other departments in the hospital I got to OB and never went back. I…*felt* her there. Like she was telling me this was where I belonged, helping women avoid her fate." She glanced up at him, the corner of her bottom lip between her teeth. "Sorry. I didn't mean to make that sound so callous, with everything you've lost."

He waved her off. "No worries. But was it just like that? From resident to a famous physician? Seems like a pretty big jump."

"Kinda like from trauma surgeon to Army Ranger and back again?" she teased.

"Touché."

She nodded, but her eyes were focused on something in the distance. Since all that was in front of them was a blank wall, it was probably something only she could see.

"Anyway, it wasn't just like that." She pulled out

a chair and gently guided Liam into it. "Put your right foot out as far as you can. Please," she added.

Liam obeyed like he was back in basic, getting put through the Crucible by a drill sergeant. The furthest he could get his leg out, though, was only a foot.

"Tell me the story," he said through gritted teeth.

"You reach toward your toes and we'll see."

He was fighting through the pain. The further he dipped his fingers, though, the more the pain dissipated, to be replaced with a not unpleasant burn.

"Good. Breathe in deep. Once more. And again... I started my practice in Detroit, actually," she told him.

"Detroit? That's about as far from Hollywood as you can get."

"You're not kidding. Now, flex your toes to the ceiling."

He did, and just as quickly the pain was back. He whistled. "Damn, this hurts. Not many celebrities there?"

"Okay, point your toes. That's it. No, no celebs. Relax your foot."

When Kelsey got up to get ice, he let himself enjoy the view. She filled out her Spandex tights nicely. So much so, his running shorts were suddenly tight around the front seam. *Damn.* There was no hiding his appreciation of her in these skimpy shorts he'd decided to wear.

"Were you there long?" he asked.

She brought back an ice pack wrapped in a towel and puffed out a breath to move her bangs out of her field of vision. It was adorable. When they just fell right down again, he fought the urge to tuck her hair back—if only to have an excuse to touch her.

They'd crossed a line somewhere in the past few days, from pleasant co-parents to friendly neighbors-slash-coworkers. Now he felt the line moving again, to something more familiar.

"Five years," she told him. "Okay, put this on your hamstring. We're gonna alternate ice and heat for the next couple hours and see if that helps."

When he groaned, she stood up and put her hands on her hips. It was sexy and intimate. Just the motivation he needed to give her brand of torture a try.

"Fine," he said. "But only if you finish your story. You know…to distract me."

She narrowed her eyes, but there was a hint of a smile tugging at the corner of her mouth. "You drive a hard bargain, but I can live with those terms."

So, she could give as much as she got. That was interesting. And a distraction he didn't need.

Never one to back down from a challenge, though, he smiled. "Deal. Now, hand over that ice pack, Doc, and keep talking."

# CHAPTER SEVEN

KELSEY HAD NEVER shared so much of her life with another person. She'd thought she known intimacy with Dex, but it had never been this easy with him. They'd never shared the telepathy that occurred when two people vibrated on the same frequency. Having Liam hear her, then ask the questions she needed him to ask to push her forward, was unnerving—and at the same time like an electric spark had shot through her.

And, odder still, rather than chiseling away at the control she kept like a stone wall around those she cared about, Liam's presence fortified it.

She told him about her mother, and then her older sister Mari, and how she'd left Detroit the minute she could… She showed him a couple pictures of Emma over the past few months, and peppered them with stories about her guilt over her father's widower status. Even the beginning of her relationship with Dex made its way into their conversation.

Liam had simply smiled and asked for more. No one had ever wanted more from her—she was a lot already.

They talked briefly about Page's time in L.A., which went better than Kelsey had hoped, given the hole Page's loss had left in all three of their lives. But her ghost would always be there. Learning to live with it and share what the woman had meant to them with Emma when she was old enough was the important thing. Hopefully, they'd have time to do that together.

And of course Liam was a model patient while they talked.

In more ways than one.

Lord help her, but catching him bent down like that in front of the cabin's front door, bare-chested and relying on nothing more than thin nylon to cover his impressive physique, had almost sent her into cardiac arrest. As a physician, she'd been intrigued by his body's reaction to the compounded stress he must have endured while he was deployed, but as a woman...?

She was captivated. Period.

Kelsey had just Velcroed the last strap on the knee brace she'd fitted Liam with when her eyes caught a scar along his jaw. She nodded at it as her fingers trailed around his thigh, checking the tightness of the brace.

"What's that from?" she asked, motioning to the hairline scar.

He shot her a look that said, *No chance*.

"Hey, I just spent the better part of my evening helping with your leg, so you won't wake up to find it torn because you let it get cold while you slept. I also shared my whole life story with you. But you can't tell me about a silly little scar?"

When his lips parted and the right corner of his mouth ticked up a notch, her own skin—chilled now that she'd cooled down from her own run—warmed up.

"Okay, but it's not as sexy a story as you think."

"I'll be the judge of that."

Good grief, why did she have the urge to grin up at him like she was a sex-starved teenager?

"Hockey."

Kelsey barked out a laugh and then recovered, but not before earning a *Told you so* shrug. "Hockey?"

"Yep. Not as sexy as a war-time scar. Not that I don't have plenty of those."

She shivered. It was like all the warm air in the room had been sucked out. "I don't think war-time scars are sexy at all. But I am curious about the hockey incident."

Liam hobbled up from the kitchen table and came back from the master bedroom with an over-sized hoodie—at least it would be oversized for her. It had a profile of a horse all in black on the front.

"You look cold," he commented, pointing down at the hair on her arms, which was standing on end. "I've…uh…never let anyone wear this before," he said, answering her unasked question.

"Are you sure it's okay?"

"Of course. I wouldn't offer if it wasn't."

"Thanks. It looks…uh…well-loved."

It felt like it, too. It was soft the way a favorite blanket might be after too many wash cycles.

"It is. It's from my first Rangers battalion. We

were the Dark Horses—which turned out to be pretty accurate, since we used jet-black mares to escape one of the hairiest situations I've ever been in."

"That sounds like something out of a movie." She smiled.

"It kinda was."

"How long were you in?"

"Special Forces? Almost ten years. Fifteen in the Army medical corps altogether."

Kelsey gulped back the wave of questions that rose up and asked, "Do you miss it? The military?"

Liam chuckled. "The clowns, maybe. The circus, not so much." He paused. "But I know that's not what you really wanted to ask."

Kelsey smiled again, her chin in her hands. "How did you…get out?"

His pupils sharpened and his jaw twitched.

"I'm sorry. I didn't mean—"

She'd told herself she didn't need to know, but sitting here in the cabin, wearing his hoodie, she felt the desire overwhelm her.

"No. It's fine. It was one of the wives of the men holding me hostage. I'd helped her kid with a broken arm and a deep chin laceration his dad gave him and she was…grateful, I guess. A month later, after I removed the kid's cast and stitches, she left the keys to the cell on the table. I got out. But the way back to safety was dicey to say the least. Anyway," he said, clearing his throat, indicating that he was done with his portion of show-and-tell, "you're right. I would go back and do it again—the escape and the risky trek home, I mean. Anything for Emma."

*Anything?* "What about Page…?"

"I wish she was here to meet her daughter, but as for her and I…? We were all but divorced when I left. I barely knew her anymore."

He shook his head and attempted a smile. Kelsey saw his mood had shifted, and though the ground they walked was stable for now, she trod carefully.

"I'm sorry. She told me you were struggling, but not how much. What happened?"

Liam paced behind the plush couch. His right leg was awkward and stiff. But at least it wouldn't give him too much trouble tomorrow.

"I told you most of it the other day. We weren't doing so well that last year—but you probably knew that much. The truth was, we were never a good fit as adults. We wanted different lives and kept waiting on the other to change their mind."

He gazed down at his feet, his eyes full of memories Kelsey could only imagine.

She exhaled the breath she'd been holding in since he started talking about Page. "Just about Emma?" she asked. "Or your careers, too?"

"Emma was actually the first thing we'd agreed on in a long time," he said.

"I'm sorry."

Liam nodded. "Thanks. It isn't like we weren't

good in the beginning. But somewhere along the line I let my fears about becoming like my father get in the way of our marriage. The shock of Page's pregnancy was the only thing capable of waking me up, I guess."

"How do you mean?"

"I was always wanting to feel healed from my past, but I wasn't really doing any work to get over my dad's neglect and my mom's turning a blind eye toward it. When Page told me about the baby I felt all that melt away. I'd started talking to the chaplain on deployment before I was captured, and some of the advice he gave me kept me afloat. Getting home for Emma became the most important thing."

"You didn't think you might reconcile with Page when you got back? If you felt better about your past?"

He shook his head. "No. We were done. But I did realize I should have let her know earlier how I felt. Not just about her, but about the life I wanted. I took the coward's way out and just left. Deployment after deployment. I told myself so many times I wouldn't become like my dad, but you could make an argument that somewhere along the line I did." He pulled his gaze up to the ceiling, then abandoned the effort, dropping sheepish eyes back to meet her gaze. "She never had a chance…"

Liam's hands were tangled in his hair. He still hadn't put on a shirt, and even though she knew it was cheap to take advantage of his vulnerability in that moment, Kelsey allowed her gaze to wander appreciatively over his frame. The scars he'd mentioned were there, but so were muscles upon muscles. He was built for the work he used to do that was for sure.

"Would you?" she asked. "Make that argument?"

"No." He smiled weakly. "It's an excuse, maybe, but not a reason. I'm trying like hell never to end up like him where it counts."

"Emma?"

He nodded. "Do you forgive Dex?"

Kelsey's eyes opened wide and she worried at her bottom lip with her teeth. The shift to her problems in that department was jarring.

"I'm not sure, to be honest. I guess… Regrets are a waste of time, even if they show you the truth. He was honest about his life, but I wasn't about mine. I won't make that mistake again."

"I'm sorry. I'd never fault someone for not being ready for parenthood, but he's an idiot."

She smiled. "That might be the nicest thing you've ever said to me," she teased, sniffing back the heat behind her eyes.

"Consider it payment for helping with my leg."

"Fair enough," she said, tucking her own legs beneath her.

It was quiet for a minute, until Liam spoke again, his voice thick and deep. "Want to know what really kills me? What I can't stop thinking about?"

He took a deep sip of his drink, then offered up

a sad smile. She nodded, even though she was worried the answer might change everything she felt about him. She'd done well to keep him at arm's length, but that was getting harder and harder to do the more time they spent together.

"I don't know if I loved Page. Like, really, truly loved her. If I had, I don't think I would have wanted to be gone as much as I was."

Kelsey didn't care about propriety anymore. She closed the distance between them with a stride and put her hands on his hips, since she couldn't reach his shoulders without standing on the tips of her toes.

"Listen to me, Liam. I'm not going to lie. Before I met you, I thought you were a jerk of the highest order."

"Thanks…" he said, a nervous chuckle shaking his chest.

"I mean, you said it yourself—you were not a good husband. You left your wife to chase your own dreams when she was pregnant and scared in a new state, being forced to rebuild herself. Right?"

Liam's jaw was set, yet he hadn't shied away. He nodded curtly.

"But can I ask you something?" she went on.

"Dare I answer? I mean, with friends like you…" He trailed off, but his gaze stayed pinned to hers.

"How is that regret serving you? Or Emma? Or even Page? If you want to be there for Emma fully, you have to face what you did and get over it. Nothing else matters anymore."

He nodded and the bottom of his eyes filled with moisture, threatening to spill. A long silence filled the room. Then, "You're right."

"I know." She smiled, relieved when he returned it. "I'm not so bad at offering advice I have no intention of taking myself. And at least I'm around to help with the odd hamstring injury."

"Of course," he said, his voice thick and breathy. "And thank you. I'll work on it. The letting it go part. I owe it to Emma. You know, she fixed everything before I'd even escaped. Knowing she was out there was why I risked running away. And that led me here—a place that's starting to feel a lot like home."

Liam gazed down at her hands, which were still on his hips. "Sorry," she muttered, taking them off.

But he reached around her back to where she'd clasped them, in case they acted of their own volition again. His hands encircled hers and drew them out, bringing them to his lips before putting them back on his waist. She saw goosepimples were raised over every inch of his very exposed, very soft skin.

"Don't be," he whispered, his voice rough with emotion. "Kelsey, I know we've got one of the most complicated stories of any co-parents I know, but thank you for keeping Emma safe…for making sure I came home to a family. I won't pretend to know why Page picked L.A., but…" A whole century seemed to pass in the pregnant pause that filled the room. "I'm glad she did."

Kelsey felt the hot sting of tears before she acknowledged the pressure in her chest. Her heart pounded against her ribcage so loud she feared it would echo against the log walls of the living room.

"Mmm-hmm," she said.

*Brilliant.*

She had an M.D. from Stanford and couldn't string together an actual sentence in that moment even if it would save her life.

There was only a thin veil of space separating her from his chest, his warmth…from his scent that was part exertion, part clean ocean air and wholly masculine. She lived in that space, concentrating on it rather than on the rough pads of his fingers that rested against her cheek, or the rapid pulse she could feel along his hip. In any other patient she'd worry he was in distress, but all she could think about was her own discomfort.

"Kelsey, look at me."

She mustered whatever shreds of courage were free-floating in her body and concentrated on meeting his gaze. Liam's eyes flashed with desire and the heat warmed her heart. As he closed the distance between their bodies she focused on what was about to happen.

Somewhere deep inside her a voice loomed ominous and loud.

*This isn't right.*

And, try as she might to silence the voice, because he felt, *oh, so good*, she worried that it was right. The last place she should be was in Liam's home…in Liam's arms.

He was Page's husband—estranged or not. And, whatever Page had been to him, she was Kelsey's friend. Besides, if this went wrong—which history showed her was all too possible—she'd lose so much more than her heart to another man. She'd lose whatever shred of self-control she had left and, worst of all, her daughter.

"Liam…" She exhaled. She waited for her mind to catch up to her body, which was crying out for him to finish what he'd started. "I have to go. I'll… I'll check in on you tomorrow to see how your leg is doing, okay?"

She pulled back from his embrace to find his chest moving through breaths as ragged as hers. At least she wasn't the only one feeling this…this *thing* that she was feeling.

*Lust. Attraction. Desire.*

*Ugh. Yes.*

And guilt. So much guilt.

Before he could argue, she gathered her keys and her phone and was out the door in a mad sprint back to her house on the other side of the property. Only when the door was safely closed behind her, and her sterile, immaculate, *safe* world was in front of her, did she realize she was still wearing his hoodie. She wouldn't have cared if it hadn't smelled exactly like him, infecting her head and her home with all sorts of inappropriate and dangerous thoughts...

Kelsey was exhausted. Bone-tired and confused.

She let the truth settle at her feet. Whether or not she was willing to admit it to herself, a certain soldier had taken her mind hostage. It was now just a matter of surviving the internment with her sanity intact.

# CHAPTER EIGHT

LIAM AVOIDED THE main house until he heard the unmistakable sound of Kelsey's car heading past his window. For five days now he'd been able to circumvent running into the woman who was stealing his sleep, more than a lion's share of his waking thoughts, and now maybe his heart. Given that they worked and all but lived together, that had been a Herculean feat.

That almost-kiss was the hottest thing he'd ever experienced. And damn if it hadn't made him want more, no matter how bad an idea that was. Not just more of her body, or her lips, but her mind, her thoughts, her smile.

But he knew how bad it would be to fall for the woman he shared custody of his daughter with. Say he did, and they gave it a shot that misfired? It would ruin everything. Emma had to come first.

Liam needed to think of something else—anything else.

He'd tried running, but the injury to his hamstring still wasn't completely healed. He'd spent as much time with Emma as his work would allow, but she'd started tilting her head and pursing her lips like Kelsey—which, of course, didn't help him put the woman out of his head. He'd even taken a twenty-four-hour shift at Mercy, hoping it would leave him so exhausted he wouldn't be able to think of anything, but he'd struck out there, too. Same with solitaire, walking the beach, playing euchre on his phone—everything but his usual tried-and-true method of relaxing, since that was exactly what he was trying to avoid.

It wasn't so much sex itself he was avoiding, but the woman he thought of when that particular desire woke him up in the middle of the night. His head warred with his body every time he dreamt of her in that cursed sports bra and tights.

Sure, he could go to some Hollywood bar and find someone to fill the loneliness with, but he didn't want that. He wanted Kelsey—for all the same reasons he couldn't have her.

She'd been good friends with his late wife.

She was a brilliant doctor.

And, God, she was amazing with Emma.

Watching them together had turned his ache for a family into a pressing need. Except even though Liam had fought through PTSD and won, now he was battling the genetic lottery and losing against his father. To be a good dad would be like an uphill walk with a boulder on his back. Nurture had failed, and if nature had anything to say about it Liam would have to work twice as hard as anyone else to be the father Emma deserved.

Which meant no distractions.

Especially not the gorgeous doc on property.

The only thing that came close to bringing him

peace and a little bit of joy was Emma—pursed lips notwithstanding. She was growing like a California poppy right in front of him. How was she seven months old already?

The once sparse tufts of hair atop her soft head were now as long as her ears. Her top two teeth had started to come in, which meant lots of frozen toys for her to gnaw on. And then there were her eyes. That pale amber, almost gold.

*Page's eyes.*

The recognition should have made him happy, but instead it filled him with regret as wide and deep as the Pacific. He should have been a better husband. He *would* be a better father. Starting with telling Emma all about Page when she was old enough to process her loss.

*Wait.* He froze as an idea came to him. *What if...?*

*Nah.*

He had enough on his plate where Kelsey was concerned. Besides, he didn't know much about this Foundation she had created. Asking her to consider expanding the charity in Page's name—maybe a couple of new locations across the country—would have to wait. But the idea sent a thrill coursing through him. It would be one hell of a legacy to give their daughter.

First things first, though.

Now the coast was clear, Liam walked over to

the main house, letting himself in with the code Kelsey had given him.

"Good morning!" Mike's voice called out from the living room. "Say good morning to your dad," he told Emma.

"Good morning, you two."

Every time one of them called him "dad" Liam's heart grew three sizes. Between the books he'd bought on parenting, and diligently studying Mike and Kelsey, he knew he'd come into his own. But that didn't mean his confidence had been a quick study. He had too many years under a negligent, dismissive father to think he could shed them at the back door and move on without fragments of historical shrapnel digging into his heart from time to time.

He skipped the coffee pot and headed straight for Emma. She crawled doggedly towards the toy Mike held out to her, her tongue stuck between her lips, her gaze focused.

*She looks like her mom.*

The thought almost knocked Liam on his butt, since the mother his brain was referring to was the beautiful doctor he'd been avoiding for days now—not Page.

*Well, hell...*

That was happening more and more often.

*You're co-parenting. Doesn't that make Kelsey her mom?*

He kissed Emma and sat beside her, giving her a foam block to play with. Gratitude washed over him.

"What brings you over here?" asked Mike. "Not that we're not thrilled to see you, but didn't you have a shift this morning?"

"I'm heading in now. Just wanted to say hi before I took off."

Liam scooped Emma off the floor and plopped her in his lap. She threw herself into his chest and tried to wrap her short, chubby arms around his torso. Warmth spread from his chest to the tips of his fingers.

"What can I do for you?" said Mike.

"I can't just want to see you two?"

Mike laughed. "You can, and you're welcome here anytime between the hours of seven-thirty and five-thirty," he said, jokingly referring to Kelsey's workday. "But your eyes say you're fixing to ask me something."

"How'd you know I was avoiding her?" Liam asked.

"Figured it out when I saw you peeking out the window like Gladys Kravitz, waiting for Kels to leave. I won't ask why you're doing it, but you're being as subtle as a rocket-propelled grenade, Cap."

Liam chuckled. "You're good, Mike. Should've gone into Intelligence. But, yeah, I was wondering if I could…"

He paused. His ask was big—really big. And ter-rifying. He'd told Kelsey he wanted to wait until Emma was more comfortable with him, but that time had come a week ago. All that stood in his way was a pair of half-limp excuses.

"I was wondering if I could have Emma tonight. At my place."

Mike didn't say anything, just regarded him from under a furrowed brow. Emma squirmed in Liam's lap until he put her down on the mat in front of him, never taking his eyes off Mike.

Finally, after an uncomfortable silence which couldn't have been more than fifteen seconds of Mike staring him down, Mike nodded.

"I was wondering if you were ever gonna get there. But it's not my place to say yes or no—which means you know who you really need to run this by."

Liam nodded and chewed on the inside of his lip.

"Can I offer you some advice?"

Liam nodded again—apparently all he was able to do.

"A phone call ain't gonna cut it."

"I figured it wouldn't."

Liam sighed out the anxiety that he'd been storing since he'd found the nerve even to con-sider taking his daughter for a night. But to feed Emma—testing the bottle temperature like Kelsey had taught him—to put her back to sleep, watch her small dreams begin to take shape… The desire welled up in him like a rogue wave.

Kelsey had told him it was his to do whenever he was ready, but if he waited for the fear to go away he'd just mess it up like his dad had—he'd never be ready.

"She in a good mood today?"

"Mmm-hmm."

"She got a busy morning?"

"Mmm-hmm."

"You gonna give me anything that might prevent me from getting my head handed to me on a medical tray?"

"Nope."

"You're a real help, Mike. Thanks."

Liam shook his head, then got up, kissing Emma on the head as he went. She gazed up at him with those big, liquid amber eyes and his strength was fortified.

"Hey."

Liam turned back around.

"Good luck. And I'll give you the same advice I gave her not too long ago."

"What's that?"

"You're on the same team. She knows you're ready for this. You've just gotta believe you are."

Liam thought about that the whole way down Highway 1. They both wanted the best for Emma. He didn't doubt that one bit.

He was interrupted in following that line of thinking any further by an incoming stream of texts.

He parked at the hospital and read them.

It's your father.

Well, obviously. His name was at the top of the text chain.

Liam was dismayed to see that the last text he'd gotten from the man said, Glad you're home, son.

Not a word in the six weeks since.

I'm just checking in. Do you need anything out there?

Liam's heart dropped into his stomach, making it twist with discomfort.

He shot back a reply.

Thanks. I'm good, though. Everything okay there?

Because his dad had never just "checked in." And he sure as hell had never offered anything to make Liam's life easier.

His dad's response took a while to come through.

Okay. Hope everything's all right. If you get a chance, can you send a picture of the little one?

Liam responded.

Sure.

He attached two of him with Emma at the beach, both of them with wide smiles and wild hair.

You look good, son. She's beautiful. Call if you ever want to talk. I'd like to catch up.

Will do.

Liam let his head fall back against the headrest with a smack.

*What the hell was that?*

He had half a mind to text back and ask if his dad had some incurable disease, since that whole thirty-second exchange was out of character.

Liam hit the steering wheel with the heel of his palm and groaned into the empty car before getting out. Weird as that conversation was, he had a stranger one still facing him.

He had to look Kelsey in the eye and convince her he was ready to be a full-time dad—with overnight stays and everything.

*You can do it.*

He stared at the outside of the OB wing. With its floor-to-ceiling windows and lush green landscaping, it was the glitziest medical facility he'd ever seen—something he could see his dad building. The inside looked more like a luxurious spa for people who wanted to hide out and recover from

plastic surgery, with its fountain in the courtyard
and security guards at the front in bespoke uni-
forms. But it was also warm and calming. He knew
Page would have wanted to give birth in a place
like this.

The air conditioning inside the lobby cooled his
skin, which was still hot with confusion over the
text conversation with his father, and the music
playing in the elevator—a gentle cello melody—
calmed his racing mind more than repeating any
mantra ever could.

By the time he got to Kelsey's floor he was
blissed out. Okay, the woman was a sorceress. No
doubt about it. And he added "brilliant" to the list
when he stepped inside her waiting room.

He whistled with appreciation. It was a combination of stark cleanliness and efficiency blended
with the cozy comfort necessary for her clientele
to feel safe. There was even a kids' playroom for
siblings, complete with two young women there
to "babysit."

*She'd thought of everything. Did Mercy know
how lucky they were to have her?*

"Liam," she said, as she strode with purpose into
the waiting room. "What are you doing here? Is
Emma okay?"

As if it were possible for him to complicate his
feelings about her anymore, he felt his heart surge
with further appreciation seeing Kelsey standing
there in her element. She looked confident in her

suit, with a sharp, fitted lab coat over it—every bit the professional her reputation suggested.

"Emma? Yeah, she's great. I just…uh…wait… Did you know I was coming?"

"My dad texted that you might be heading over before your shift. And then Ben, my security manager, said he saw you get in the elevator. I put two and two together," she teased.

He forced a laugh that sounded more like a cackle.

*Shoot me now. If I hadn't tried to kiss her just days after throwing her world upside down maybe I wouldn't feel so awkward now. Hindsight and karma are real pains in the—*

"Anyway, what can I do for you?"

"Of course." Liam should have felt at ease, especially given his surroundings, but a nagging feeling of imposter syndrome crept in. "Can I…uh… talk to you for a minute?"

*Like, in the trauma wing, so I can think clearly?*

"Sure. Come on back. I have about twenty minutes until my next appointment."

"That should be plenty. I start at nine."

Liam followed her into an open space with an oak desk and about a dozen twenty-by-thirty photos of babies that must have been taken just after their births.

"Those are incredible," he said, pointing to the series.

"Thanks. One of my moms in Detroit took the

first one, to say thanks, and I commissioned her to do the rest. Her name is Angie. And I have to say, to date, they're my favorite gifts from a patient."

"Angie ever do anything with her photography? She's pretty talented."

Kelsey walked over to one of the pictures and sent Liam a look filled with emotion. His training said it was regret, if not pain. Maybe both.

"I helped her open a studio here in L.A. She's made quite a name for herself. Some of her work will be featured at the Gold Fleece Foundation dinner at the end of the month, actually." Kelsey paused, her gaze falling to the floor. "This one is Emma…"

Liam's stomach sank down to about where Kelsey's gaze was pinned. When he looked closely at the photo he could see the unmistakable heart-shaped birthmark on Emma's thigh that he saw every time he changed her diaper.

"She's so…small."

"If I remember right, she was just shy of six pounds when that photo was taken. It was going to be my gift for Page."

Liam felt his past slipping away from him one day at a time. Page was gone, taking Emma's birth story along with her, not to mention a lifetime of raising Emma with him as a co-parent. He couldn't fix that, nor his absence for her first six months. In the scope of Emma's whole life, he hadn't been gone long. But looking at her now, minutes after her birth, seeing the small and tremendous ways she'd changed, he felt an unquenchable ache grow like a cancer in his stomach.

Not because of Kelsey, who'd saved him from losing Emma altogether, but because of the injustice of...*everything*.

Much of his anger was aimed at himself—at his gnawing guilt for leaving Emma to begin life without a parent present, and for the loss Emma would always endure for never getting to meet her mother. Then there was added guilt for his growing affection and lessening indifference to Kelsey, the woman at the center of his loss. It didn't help that now she took his hand and rubbed circles into the pad of his thumb, centering him and washing away most of the sadness.

"Can I have this? Or if not this, then a copy? I'd love to hang it, since it's the earliest picture I have of her."

"Of course. I'll have it brought to your house today. I'm sorry I didn't give it to you sooner. I just didn't know how much you'd want to know. Or see."

He didn't know either, but this was good, so maybe more would be, too.

"I think I need to see it. I'd love to see more candid shots, too. Like you showed me the other night."

Kelsey laughed—a light, airy sound he'd come to look forward to.

"I have...um...quite a few. I tend to overindulge

where photos of Emma are concerned, so thank God for digital cameras. Maybe we could make some time tonight to look through them?"

*Tonight... Hadn't he come here asking something particular about tonight? Oh, yeah, an overnight with Emma.*

He recalled his dad's infamous saying: *There are more than two ways to suture a cut.*

"I'd love that. Can you bring Emma? I'd love us to spend time with her together. Like, you and me."

For some reason his intentions had shifted, and having Emma to himself that evening wasn't as important as having the three of them together.

Kelsey's face turned that same shade of red he associated with her when she was embarrassed. Or excited. What color might her paint-by-emotion skin have turned if they'd followed through on that kiss? Or if they'd taken it further...? He desperately wanted to know.

"I'm looking forward to it. Come to the house. I'll cook."

"And I'll bring the drinks."

"You off at six?" she asked.

He nodded. "Yep. Home twenty minutes after that."

*Home.* Huh...he hadn't used that word to describe a place in years.

Kelsey smiled and opened her office door, indicating that their time together was up.

Just in time, too—since he couldn't contain the

smile on his face any longer if he tried. He was looking forward to tonight, too. Perhaps a little too much, considering he didn't have a clue how Kelsey felt about him.

Hopefully this evening would shed some clarity on that, too. Because right now he could use a shove in one direction or another.

# CHAPTER NINE

KELSEY WATCHED LIAM walk out through the lobby on the third-floor mezzanine, her heart pounding against her ribcage so strongly she worried it might crack a bone.

*Did he just ask me on a date? Because it seemed like he did.*

The second question was how did she feel about it?

Her heart was pretty clear on its stance, but her head spun through the myriad ways this was a bad idea. Liam was the widower of one of her colleagues—a colleague who'd become very dear to her. He was the biological father of her soon-to-be adopted daughter. And every time she was with him she lost all sense of right and wrong—only spending more time with him mattered.

Even being his friend was a liability.

Her phone buzzed in the pocket of her lab coat and she reached for it, swiping it without glancing at who was calling. Her gaze was still laser-focused on the front door and the beautiful backside of the man she might or might not have a date with that evening, who was now chatting with the husband of one of her patients.

"This is Dr. Gaines. How can I help you?"

The heavy breathing on the other end of the line sent red flags pinging against Kelsey's brain. It was one of her moms and she was in distress. Kelsey slipped through her mental Rolodex of names of women who were close to their due date while she issued instructions.

"Okay, I hear you. I need you to take one long, slow breath for me, okay?"

The patient on the other line breathed in, but the sound that came out was more like a wheeze. Pulmonary edema? If it was, Kelsey needed to see this patient *now*.

She looked down at the screen on her phone. It was a Denver area code. Denver? Which of her patients was in…?

*Nora.*

Nora lived just outside Denver, but was here in L.A. till the birth of her daughter—which was going to be today, most likely.

"Is this Nora?" asked Kelsey.

"Y-y-yes."

Kelsey expelled her own frantic breath. Each time she had a patient in distress worry filtered through her veins, speeding up her actions, focusing her thoughts. She understood that there was science behind this—that it was adrenaline—but knowing her body wouldn't betray her in stressful moments like this calmed her mind just enough to hold that edge. Then her training and years of experience took over, like it did now. Training that told her she couldn't do this alone.

She covered the receiver with her hand and called down to the first floor.

"Liam!" His gaze shot up to hers and his expression hardened. "I need you."

He nodded, said something quick to the family he was talking to, and then took the stairs to the mezzanine three at a time.

Kelsey put the phone on speaker as Liam reached her side. One of his hands rested on the balcony rail in front of them, while the other rested supportively on her shoulder. As if his palm was actually a heating pad, she felt warmth spread from his palm down her arm and across her back. It calmed her breathing and steadied her pulse.

"Tell me what's going on, Nora."

She and Liam bent over the phone as Nora's halted speech came in short bursts and made a hissing sound when she exhaled. Liam nodded knowingly at Kelsey and his thumb rubbed her shoulder blade. The heat coming from his hand turned her liquid. Did he even realize he was doing that?

"Are you at the hotel?" she asked.

"Yes..."

Kelsey called up the Foundation hotel's address in her patient files, pointed it out to Liam.

He flagged down a nurse. "Can you do me a favor?"

"Of course, Dr. Everson," she replied.

"Good—thanks. I need you to get an ambulance

to this hotel room. Tell them to have oxygen on hand. Patient in pulmonary distress."

He looked to Kelsey, who finished the history.

"She's thirty-nine weeks pregnant. No family history of respiratory issues, no allergies. Thanks."

The nurse nodded to Kelsey.

"Alone…" Nora whispered. "Mom is out. The store…"

"Okay. We've already alerted emergency medical services, and we'll call her. There'll be a trauma team waiting for you when you get here."

Liam cut in, his voice serious but kind. "Nora, I'm Dr. Everson, a trauma physician here at Mercy. This is what I need from you. I need you to lay down on your right side with your right arm raised above your head. Take long, slow breaths and stay on the phone with me, okay?"

"Okay…"

Kelsey let out a sigh of relief when Nora's breathing sounded more regular.

*Thank you*, she mouthed to Liam.

He nodded and sent her a kind smile.

She borrowed his strength.

"Dr. Gaines?"

"Yes, Nora?"

"I'm scared."

"Oh, there's nothing to worry about. Just a little hiccup. We're going to get you squared away at the hospital and then you'll get to meet sweet Evan a little early. Sound good?"

"Mmm…" Nora whispered.

Kelsey hung up the phone after the paramedics had arrived at Nora's suite and informed her and Liam they had the patient en route.

"Will you talk me through her case?" Liam asked as they left the OB wing.

His pace was quick, but he slowed down when he saw Kelsey struggling to keep up.

"Are you sure?" she asked, stopping in the hallway before the doors leading to the ER.

Liam paused and looked back at her, his eyes filled with concern.

"It's the same complication as—"

"No," he said, shaking his head. "I don't mean to cut you off, but we can't think that way if we're going to save Nora. A pulmonary embolism is risky, no matter what."

He was right. But what Liam didn't know was that it was the complication that had silently killed her mother just minutes after Kelsey had taken her first breath.

"Nora is a different patient with different biometrics than Page—so, please, talk me through her case so I can do my best to save her."

"She's high risk polycystic ovary syndrome, which led to three pregnancy losses before this one. She's been on bedrest, but I'm worried about—"

"Preeclampsia. I agree. Go on."

Kelsey ran through the pregnancy losses Nora had experienced, the early bleeding at the beginning of her term, and the high blood pressure that sent her to complete bedrest the last two weeks.

"Another Hollywood socialite coming in with a camera crew?" he asked.

Kelsey shook her head, even though Liam couldn't see it.

He shoved open the ER doors and grabbed a gown for each of them, helping Kelsey into hers. Watching his measured confidence in the tension-filled space buoyed her again. She didn't like being down here unless she had to be, preferring the tranquility and calm procedure of her birthing suites, but with Liam by her side the incoming traumas, the constant beeping of machinery, and the personnel rushing through with crash carts wasn't half as nerve-racking.

"No. She's one of my Gold Fleece patients. That's my charity...the one Page was on the board for, for a while," she added for clarity.

"Got it. I'm aware of the basics of your Foundation, but maybe you can fill me in on the specifics later. Any family for Nora except her mom?"

He washed his hands in the basin sink and held them up to air dry. She followed his lead and did the same.

"Just her mom."

"They're local?"

"No. The Foundation has put them up in L.A. before the birth."

He shot her a glance. "It's not just for local women?"

Kelsey shook her head. "Not necessarily. We support any woman who qualifies in the last trimester if they don't have adequate insurance coverage. It's great, but I wish we had an even bigger reach. The Foundation covers all the hospital bills and incidentals so the families don't have to worry. I just wish there was more I could do for women who can't come to L.A."

"Why can't you?"

"Who would run something big like that? I can't be in two places at once, and there's no one else I trust."

Liam's gaze was kind, but unreadable. His hazelnut-colored eyes were half hidden behind his furrowed brow, but his jaw wasn't tight with any stress.

"How do you pick the patients?"

"Through the Foundation's board," she said.

"Which Page was on?"

"Exactly. We choose patients through local news stories, word of mouth—that sort of thing. We found Nora when her husband's story was highlighted on the local news."

"Military?"

"Woodland firefighter. His company was flown in from Oregon. He died protecting homes and families around L.A. from the wildfires. Nora didn't even know she was pregnant when he was killed."

Liam just nodded, looking more and more like he had something he wanted to say. But before Kelsey could ask him to tell her what he was thinking, the doors to the ER bay opened and paramedics rushed in.

"Dr. Gaines?" one of them shouted.

"That's me. You've got Nora? How's she doing?"

The paramedic read off the vitals. They weren't great, but they hadn't deteriorated either, which was encouraging. The blue lips and pale discoloration of Nora's skin were strong indicators of edema, but could also be symptoms of something else.

"Kelsey," Liam said, "she's your patient, but I'd like to get a full work-up in case the issue is affecting her ability to deliver."

Kelsey nodded. She'd never shared a patient's care after Page, but this was different. She trusted Liam.

"That works for me. I'll concentrate on getting her prepped for delivery, and if either of us has issues we'll reassess?"

"Sounds good."

The same two nurses from Liam's first day were at their side in a flash.

"What do you need from us?" they asked.

"Good to see you both. Tina, I need you to run a cardio and echo and get an MRI of her lungs. Susan, can you get OR Two set up for me in case surgery is necessary?" Liam asked.

"Yes, Liam," Susan replied.

Only a brief moment's pause slowed Liam and Kelsey's pace as they gathered the results of the tests over the next hour or so. They worked in sync, like they'd been a team for years, not minutes.

When the tests came back Liam bent over her shoulder, reading the MRI results.

"There's a bleed," he said. "On her C-4 vertebrae."

Kelsey nodded. "Two—look," she said, pointing to a spot inside the uterus. "This has got to be handled or we'll lose the baby."

Liam shook his head. "But if we don't address the spine, we'll lose the mother."

A shudder ran through Kelsey like a rogue winter wave.

*Not again.*

"Okay. I trust you. But I'd like to monitor the infant the whole time, and if anything changes I'm going in. It's in Nora's Advance Directive—save her child if there's a choice that has to be made."

It was an impossible choice she hoped they didn't have to make.

Just three miles away was everything she cared about, probably swaddled and sucking on a pacifier, hopefully dreaming sweet dreams of playing in the surf and snuggling with her dad and Kelsey. It was enough to make Kelsey hesitate for the briefest of seconds.

Emma was her whole world, and she could have been taken from her in a millisecond if she'd snipped one wrong cord or nicked one blood vessel she shouldn't have. Even though the physician she'd recommended had run one last echo, it hadn't been enough to save Page.

Every time her mind wandered to Liam, it wasn't to the potential custody suit they might end up with, or how he might have saved Page if he'd been there, but to the way he'd looked at her when she'd been in the cabin. The way he'd almost kissed her. How gentle he was with Emma. And now here he was, working steadily alongside her. She knew he wouldn't let anything happen to Nora.

Hours later, Kelsey handed a healthy, nine-pound, four-ounce boy to the nurse while Liam closed the spinal incision. It had been touch-and-go for a minute, with the infant's heart rate dropping below what was safe, but an intervention from Liam at the last minute had saved Nora from Page's fate and made sure Kelsey could perform an emergency Cesarean to save the child.

It looked like both mother and baby were out of the woods, and Kelsey sent up a small prayer of thanks to whichever deity was on call tonight.

*Thank you for protecting this mom. This family.*

Nora had told her at her last checkup that she was naming him Evan after another firefighter who had been killed with her husband. It was perfect— a balancing of the scales and a reminder of why the Gold Fleece Foundation was so vital.

Kelsey waved Tina and Susan over. "I want

hourly updates—and please page me if anything goes wrong. I don't want any on-call doc handling Nora and her baby. Only our team until she's safe at home—understood?"

"Of course. Great job, Kelsey. Thank Liam, too."

"Thanks. I will."

She waited for Liam to clean up and checked her email—mostly rescheduled appointments from patients she hadn't been able to see because she'd been pulled into this emergency surgery. All things she could attend to tomorrow. But she wasn't ready to go home. Not yet.

"You did good in there," Liam's voice said from behind her.

She turned around to find him in a clean pair of scrubs, his hair glistening with moisture.

She nodded, her throat dry all of a sudden. "Thanks. You, too. I'm… I'm glad you were there."

"You heading home?"

The way he said it—*home*—made her think of what that might look like: going back to a complete family, including a man who would love and support her instead of running at the first sign of something that made him uncomfortable. A man like Liam. If only he were any other man and she any other woman.

"Not yet. I'm going to catch up on some paperwork here and make sure I'm ready for tomorrow. I've got double the work now I've pushed back today's schedule."

"Okay. Want me to wait?"

"No. I won't be long. Give Emma a kiss from me."

He put a hand on her shoulder again and this time it sent Kelsey's pulse north of one-eighty.

When he left, walking towards the parking lot, his words and touch still haunted her, and she allowed herself the freedom to release all the emotions she'd been harboring for the past seven hours. The past seven months, really. Half an hour she sat there, letting out the loss and the fear and the pain so she didn't take it home with her.

What remained was pride. She'd trusted Liam with her patient and it had been okay. She was okay, and Emma would be, too.

Another half an hour and she was finally ready to stand up, head to her car.

When a stream of texts came in, she dried her eyes with the back of her hands and checked them. They were from her dad.

Heading to bed, hun. Liam and Emma are at the cabin.

Have a good night and see you after work tomorrow. Don't forget I'm fishing tomorrow morning. Won't be there when you get up. Liam's got it covered.

Love you, Bug.

Kelsey smiled, but just as quickly the smile fell. In the chaos of caring for Nora, she'd completely forgotten about her promise to show Liam pictures of his daughter. *Their* daughter. But not a cell in her body had enough stored energy to put in that effort tonight, though.

She pulled into her property ten minutes later and drove straight to Liam's cabin, with hopes of rescheduling. She knocked, but instead of greeting her at the door he whispered loud enough for her to hear through the open window.

"It's open."

Kelsey let herself in—and simultaneously had the wind knocked out of her like she'd been struck across the chest with a log.

On the couch by the fire—which was lit, offering the only light in the room—sat a shirtless Liam, with Emma asleep on his chest, an empty bottle and *The Very Hungry Caterpillar* open beside them. Every muscle in his arms and torso was taut and visible beneath the sleeping infant.

Kelsey's stomach roared with heat, and longing, liquid and hot, spread through her like lit gasoline. She tried to swallow, but something was stuck in her throat.

"Hi," she whispered. "You two look so sweet."

"Thanks. She just went down after a bottle and some avocado."

"Wow. Hungry girl. Where'd you get the avocado?" she asked.

"I blended it along with some carrots and peas and froze it in little cubes to defrost when she's up here with me."

"You…made your own baby food?"

"Don't act so surprised. I told you I was going to buy a book. I may have picked up a couple tips along the way."

"I'm impressed," Kelsey said.

Somewhere along the line he'd become a dad— and a good one at that.

"Want me to take her?"

Liam shook his head, a soft smile playing on his lips. His posture and his gesture both suggested he was as relaxed as they come, but his eyes… His fluid gold and chestnut gaze melted Kelsey right on the spot. They were a different version of the eyes she'd seen in the ER, when she'd mentioned her Gold Fleece Foundation. Was it respect she'd seen in them then? Now the look he sent her was hungry. Needy, yet in control.

He patted the seat next to him and Kelsey didn't think twice about kicking off her shoes, tucking her legs underneath her, and leaning against Liam's shoulder. Though he wasn't facing the fire, it was warm, but she resisted sinking the rest of the way against the welcome heat.

She bent down and kissed Emma's pudgy arm, marveling at the way it seemed made of clouds and yet was so solid.

"Tell me how you're feeling," he said.

The command was so simple, so delicately put, she couldn't refuse.

"Today was hard. Long. Exhausting and soul-sucking. But also beautiful… Anyway, I'm sorry I'm so late. Did you eat? I hope you didn't wait for me."

"I did, and I saved you a plate. I also poured you a glass of wine. It's on the counter."

God, she wanted both—the food and the wine—but moving from her spot on the couch was impossible.

"I know you wanted to look at—"

"Shh… We'll do it another time—and before you try, I don't need an apology."

She looked up at him—a mistake if she was hoping to maintain her composure. Because, good grief, Liam was handsome—more so this close up. His crooked smile…his strong jawline with the scar that ran parallel at the edge of it…his long, black lashes… Emma had those same beautiful eyelashes, the lucky girl.

"Well, too bad," she teased. "I am sorry—and for bringing up what happened to Page at the hospital. I'm never sure when it's okay to mention her."

Liam shook his head and smoothed Emma's hair. Her mouth was open, her small, full lips in the shape of a perfect heart, just like her birthmark.

Kelsey's heart swelled against her chest.

"I actually think I need to hear more about it, if

it's okay with you? Your dad said something about you having nightmares?"

Kelsey shook her head. "Not since…"

*Not since you showed up.*

"Not for a while," she hedged. "I don't mind talking about her."

"Okay. Then I want to know."

Kelsey took a deep breath and dove in, explaining everything from her budding friendship with Page to Emma's delivery and what had gone wrong, and her guilt over letting Page out of her care even though her complications had been too great, too severe, for her to be saved regardless.

"It's not your fault," Liam told her. "Please don't feel bad for not doing what would have been impossible to do."

"Thank you. I've been carrying that guilt with me for so long now, but it's not that simple. I'd offered to take her on as a Gold Fleece client, since you two had separated and she lived in L.A. And your dad—"

"Let me guess. He didn't offer to help."

"Not at all."

"Kels, you did everything you could. I'm so sorry you're carrying that, and I don't blame you— not for any of it."

She pulled up the letter Page had written on her phone, asking Kelsey to care for Emma. "Can I read you this?"

Liam never said a word, just nodded and wrapped his arm around Kelsey's shoulders.

*"'You're my best friend, and I can't imagine my daughter growing up with anyone but you,'"* Kelsey read through her tears.

Liam kissed the top of her head, much in the tender way he did with Emma.

"I agree," he whispered.

Kelsey was struck again by how much they'd look like a loving family to an outsider. The problem was, it was starting to feel that way to Kelsey, too—a feeling she had no right to be having. For her, caring for Emma was a learn-as-you-go adventure, and Liam's temporary time in L.A. was an obstacle to that.

Watching him with her was enchanting, but the way she was starting to feel was perilously close to *love*. And that emotion was as out of control as one could get. And control was a necessity in this tenuous co-parenting situation.

They sat in silence, breathing in unison, until Liam cleared his throat.

"How did Page end up on the Gold Fleece board?"

Kelsey's cheeks felt like they were against the open flame in the fireplace they'd gotten so hot. "She applied when she read about what I was doing in *Military Spouse Magazine*. She was the best thing for the Mercy nursing staff and for the charity as well. Her energy was infectious."

"I remember… I'm glad she got some of that back with me gone. She didn't exactly thrive in our marriage." He paused. "But how could she become a patient? Wasn't that a conflict of interest?"

"We took her on as a patient when…" The words felt thick, salty on her tongue.

"When…?"

"When you filed for divorce. She wasn't able to go to a military hospital anymore, your father wouldn't help, and her health insurance here wasn't enough. She quit the board at my urging, so she could be covered by a Foundation grant."

"Wow. I had no idea it'd been so tough for her." Regret laced his words.

"She was a tough woman."

"Yes. She was. May I ask why you started the Foundation?"

"That's a more complicated answer. I've got this reputation as OB to the rich and famous…"

Saying it aloud made her cringe. Had she willingly cultivated this life for herself? Still, Liam just nodded, his eyes kind, but concentrating.

"And it's great; it affords me a lifestyle I could never have imagined growing up. But it's not how or why I started practicing, so I made a commitment to get some of that back."

"You didn't have this in Detroit?" he asked.

"Nope. It was as stark a change from there to here as it could be. There I had low-income families, at-risk pregnancies due to lack of access to healthcare. You name it… I actually loved it. I felt like I was doing something good. But then *she* showed up, almost nine months into her pregnancy—the star of that reality show that went viral…the one with the family who became influencers and took over half the world… Anyway, she went into premature labor with preeclampsia. It was a mess, but she and the baby were fine. God, that baby must be a preteen now…"

She shook her head in disbelief.

"Anyway, she apparently liked how I handled the birth and demanded I visit her here in L.A. She paid me to come out—more money than I'd ever seen in my account at one time—and the rest is history where that's concerned."

"You stayed out here, then?"

Kelsey nodded. "It's been ten years. Three for the Gold Fleece. I just wish I could do more. Mercy is a standalone hospital, and with it being small, I can control the outcomes. It's actually my dream to open satellite clinics in other cities."

"That's not the first time you've mentioned that. And wouldn't it help more women?"

"Yes, but I'm not sure how it would work."

*Or who I could trust to co-run the program.*

"Maybe we could brainstorm some ideas one night."

"I'd like that very much."

And she would. Dex had never wanted to talk

shop, and she missed the give and take of ideas and solutions between friends.

She rested her elbows on her knees and let her chin fall to her hands. Liam ran the tips of his fingers along her spine. Shivers followed in their wake and her whole body felt like an exposed nerve.

*Friends.* Or perhaps…more?

Emma let out a soft cry and he comforted her with a gentle shushing sound. He was so good with her.

"You wanted all this so other women wouldn't go through what your mom did?"

She nodded. He understood, and that realization ripped through her like a shot of pure adrenaline.

"Taking on women who don't have access to good healthcare is noble. I'm glad Page had you by her side. Especially knowing now how the divorce left her…*without*. It kills me, knowing how rough the pregnancy was on her and that I couldn't do a damn thing to help her. You did, though. I see it now—why she chose you for Emma."

"She meant so more to me than just a colleague or a patient, Liam. I hope you know that."

"Kelsey, look at me. Please."

Kelsey opened her mouth to speak, to brush off his kindness with self-deprecation, but he shook his head.

"No. I mean it. Don't deflect."

He saw right through her, as if she was nothing but a transparent layer of cells.

"Here, come with me."

She didn't break his gaze as he got up, extending the hand that was not holding Emma. She took it and followed him into the second bedroom, just next to the master. He flipped on the light and she gasped.

*What had he done? More importantly... How? And when?*

"When did you do all this?"

Because he worked as much as her, and when he wasn't on shift he was glued to his daughter's side.

He shrugged. "I had help. I may have weaseled your dad into being my second set of hands. But I... I wanted to. I figure I missed out on the first round of all this, and every father's got to struggle with a crib at least once in his life, right?"

She nodded, struck silent.

*Because it was so much more than a crib.*

There was a mural of various zoo animals spanning all three walls, and Emma's name was painted above the crib—the very well-constructed crib. In the corner were three connected shelves, filled with kids' books and plush toys. By the crib he'd even added the same kind of rocker she had in every room at the main house, with a fully stocked changing table behind it.

"Is it okay? Your dad seemed to think so…but I defer to you, since you're her mom."

"It's…perfect."

*He'd called her Emma's mom.*

Her pulse was close to tachycardic, slowed only by the memory of Page, of what had been lost so Kelsey could have this moment. A need to honor that loss grew in her with urgency, but she needed more time to figure out how to do so in a way that Page would have appreciated.

"The boutique furniture stores downtown were our best friends. I think we've got gold status there," he chuckled.

She couldn't join him in laughing. Something else—an emotion she couldn't name—had welled up inside her, pushing the stress, the exhaustion, the reticence away.

Liam gently laid Emma down in the crib, caressing her cheek. Then he walked over to Kelsey, sliding the heel of his palm along her cheek in a much less innocent manner. She leaned her head against him, letting his support carry her. His palm was damp…or her cheek was. She couldn't tell which.

*Gratefulness.*

That was what she was feeling as she looked around the room. She was so very grateful to Liam for this unexpected gift—for the room…for allowing her to co-parent with him…

For the way he made her feel.

"Are you okay?" he asked.

She nodded.

His voice was rough, lined with emotion. "Why are you crying?"

*Was she? Because she wasn't sad. Not even close.*

"I didn't know I was, but I'm okay. No, I'm better than okay. Thank you, Liam. What you've done here is incredible."

"It's nice to see you happy."

"I'm more than happy, Liam. I'm—"

She was lost for how to finish that sentence, how to explain what all this meant to her, what he was starting to mean to her. If this was what chaos felt like, she wouldn't mind relenting to it.

She didn't get a chance before his lips crushed hers, his tongue separating them to explore her mouth.

This time, she didn't push him away.

*This is how you can show him what he means to you. In a way he'll understand.*

They might have complicated pasts, exes who had done too much damage, and a world of other problems on the other side of that kiss, but it wasn't enough to turn him away. Come hell or high water, she was giving in to this—whatever *this* was—tonight.

She'd wrestle with the consequences in the morning.

# CHAPTER TEN

WHEN KELSEY LAY down and arched her back, Liam couldn't keep his grin from spreading across his face.

Her skin was a map of pleasure, laid out just for him. With peaks and valleys rife with tender, warm places for him to explore. He'd have happily spent eight months as *her* prisoner... She was spread out on top of his bed, clad only in a thin strip of lace underwear, and he couldn't keep his eyes or his hands off her.

"You're stunning," he told her, kissing her raised hipbone.

Her groan of pleasure ignited something he'd thought was long dead and gone from his heart.

"Am not—but I like that you think so."

He growled, rubbing his thumb along her swollen bottom lip. "You don't get to tell me what I think... only what you want."

"I want your lips," she said, looking up at him with eyes thick with lust.

"Where?" he asked. "Show me."

Because he was here to serve at her pleasure. She pointed to her belly button and he kissed it. Then she pointed to the top of her stomach, which he happily licked, eliciting a giggle from her.

When she put a finger on each breast he didn't hesitate to oblige her, taking each in his mouth and giving them the attention they deserved. She bucked beneath him, eliciting small cries. Hopefully that meant he was on the right track.

"Please… I can't anymore… It's too much…" she breathed out on an exhale.

He contemplated ignoring her request, since her hands were still tangled in his hair and her eyes were bright with desire, but finally he sat back on his heels and appraised her. She really was the most beautiful woman he'd ever seen.

Every inch of Kelsey's body was a hot spot. Each moan meant he was doing something right. Each kiss she peppered his skin with lit a path of flames down to the part of him that desperately wanted in on the action. But he had his boxer briefs on—a travesty as far as she was concerned, it seemed, since she kept pulling at them, trying to tug them off.

"Nope. Not right now. Now is about you."

"You're so stubborn," she whispered against his neck.

Her breath was warm against his cool skin. He pulled her closer and nibbled on the soft area beneath her earlobe.

"Are you complaining, Doctor?"

"Mmm-mmm… I would never…"

The last word escaped from her lips on a whisper as his thumb slipped between the thin swathe of fabric along her hip and her skin. He moved to her other earlobe and trailed his tongue along it.

"I want to make you scream with pleasure, Doc. So tell me how I'm doing as I go, okay?"

She nodded as he pinned her arms over her head.

"And I'm gonna take my time," he said, moving his mouth across her collarbone and down the curve of her breast.

Her nod gained velocity and she worried at her bottom lip with her teeth. It drove him nuts to watch, not to take over with his teeth on her mouth, but this was about her. Making her happy.

Liam bent in front of Kelsey, teasing her open with his tongue. He traced circles at her center, sucking and pulling her into him.

"I need you inside me," she moaned.

Not one to deny a woman's request, he stripped down and sheathed himself in a condom before sliding into Kelsey's tight, wet warmth.

"Take me, Liam," she whispered.

Only their mouths and hands and tongues mattered, coming together to ravish each other. The fire in the living room had gone out who knew how long ago, but between the central heating and their physical exertion the bedroom was plenty warm enough.

He thrust deeper, until they filled each other, repeating until Kelsey arched her back and cried out with pleasure. Liam let himself release the desire he'd been holding in so they came together. Sated, he rolled over and looked at her.

Days and weeks of desire were strewn along

with their discarded clothes on the floor. The bed-sheets weren't even on the bed anymore, and nei-ther would there be any talk of what came before this or how they were going to handle things in the morning.

"I could do this all night. Make you come over and over, until you scream my name loud enough for the people on Hollywood Boulevard to hear."

He planned on doing it, too. That was until an unmistakable cry came from the room next to theirs.

Rather than be dismayed, Kelsey laughed.

"Is that how you plan to make me scream your name? By sending a hungry infant my way?" she teased, getting up and pulling on his discarded but-ton-down shirt.

Liam smacked her playfully on her backside and jumped up too.

"Don't get up," he told her, laughing as he pulled on his jeans. "You lay there and think about all the things I can do to you when I get back. You might even consider taking a power nap. Because you, Dr. Gaines, are gonna need it."

Kelsey propped herself up on her elbows and the sight of her there, in nothing but his button-down flannel shirt, made his stomach flip. Had his stomach ever done that before? He didn't mind it—not when it came with a woman looking up at him like that.

Liam bent down and kissed her again, opening

her mouth with his, until Emma's cries increased in intensity.

"I'll be back," Liam said in a mock Arnold Schwarzenegger voice.

She giggled and snatched a pillow from the floor, whacking him on the shoulder with it.

"Go get our daughter. She's not going to get any quieter."

Liam jogged out of the room, feeling lighter than he had in months. Years, even.

*Our daughter.*

The same words said to him two weeks ago would have shocked him. But now... Now they fit like a worn set of scrubs...comfortable and familiar. Something had shifted the night before— maybe had been slowly shifting, like a glacier down a ravine, since the day he'd met Kelsey. His failings as a son, a husband, and an Army medic had disappeared beneath the feel of Kelsey's arms around him. He'd been enough for her. And that was a start. As long as he kept on showing up for her and Emma, maybe it could be the start of something wonderful. Something very unlike what he'd grown up with.

He rounded the corner into what he'd turned into Emma's room and came up short.

"Whoa, there, Em. Stay there. Don't move."

Emma was standing up for the first time, clinging to the crib's railing and shaking it like the Hulk.

*"Kelsey..."* he hissed. If he yelled and she let go, and Kelsey missed this, he'd never forgive himself.

Liam got out his phone to take a video, but was distracted when he saw three missed calls from Texas. Each of them was ignorable until he saw the text from his father that came with them. The time stamp said three forty-three a.m., and the contents merely read:

Just want to talk. Call me when you get a chance.

As Emma giggled and bounced on her feet, Liam groaned. Just the sight of a Texas number on his cell felt like a violation of the space he'd cultivated for himself. But three calls and a text?

*No.* Not today. Kelsey had told him how she'd asked his father to consider taking Emma, since he was her paternal grandfather, and he'd turned her down—turned *Liam's daughter* down—the man could wait.

"Kelsey!" Liam called out again. "Come here. Quick."

Kelsey came sprinting into the room, her face pale with terror. "Is she okay? What's—?"

When her gaze settled on Emma in her crib she squealed with delight, her hands flying to her mouth. Emma seemed to take this as her cue to really show off and squealed back, bouncing on her toes, even lifting one leg for a moment.

"She's *standing*!" Kelsey exclaimed.

"I know. I actually got a little choked up when I walked in. How is she so big already?"

Kelsey shook her head and gave a little sniff that let Liam know he wasn't alone in his awe.

"Come here, you."

He wrapped his arms around Kelsey like it was the most natural thing in the world to do. But as Kelsey nuzzled her way closer to his chest his mind warred with his heart. This felt so damn right. But would starting a relationship pull his focus from Emma? Especially a relationship with the woman at the center of his tangled web of history?

*I'll take it slow*, he told himself. *If it does, I can always course-correct.*

He'd figured out how to be a good dad by observing and reading and practicing the hell out of it. So why couldn't he practice being a good partner?

*Because being a partner isn't on your approved list of things to do to avoid becoming like your father. Remember what your dad told you about that?*

How could he forget?

*"You may think you know but, son, you don't have a damn clue what a wife needs. It's not just hugs and pats on the back, I'll tell you that much,"* his father had said, just before Liam had eloped

with Page. *"You'll be back in a month, begging for your job and the name of a good divorce attorney."*

His dad had been right. Only five weeks into his marriage with Page, he'd wondered, *What did I do?*

He'd hated his dad—hated him for never being there unless it was to say, *"I told you so."* So, Liam had never given him the chance. He sucked it up and kept right on deploying, like being absent would fix anything.

But Kelsey wasn't Page, and he wasn't the man who bowed to his father's demands anymore. Nor was he going to run from something he wanted to do...*needed* to do.

Because he *liked* being part of a family.

*This* family...

"This is incredible," she whispered.

He felt the vibrations of her voice on his chest and smiled.

"It is," he replied, kissing the top of her ear. So much of what he felt physically for Kelsey stemmed from watching her with Emma. "She's amazing, and so are you. Hey, I'm gonna grab some water. Want some?"

Still holding her hand to his chest, Kelsey pulled him back into her, so they were pressed together, reigniting the desire he'd barely been able to tamp down.

"You're pretty okay, too," she teased. "Seriously, though. I like this," she said, pointing back and forth between their bodies.

He smiled, holding his breath so he didn't inhale the scent of cinnamon and salt lacing her skin. He needed a second, just a breath and a moment, to tame his growing feelings for her, but she made it so damn hard.

"I agree. Here—take a video so we have this memory forever," he said, handing Kelsey his phone.

"Hurry back, Doc. I have plans for you once I'm done feeding Emma."

She smiled, her eyes warm and inviting.

It took every ounce of his strength to walk away from her.

That didn't bode well for taking it slow.

*"You're asking for it again, Liam."*

He shut down his dad's voice that acted like a snarky conscience in the back of his head. But it persisted.

*"You'll lose her if you won't let yourself be vulnerable and you'll lose Emma, too."*

No. He wouldn't. He could do vulnerability—especially with her. Whatever passion, intimacy, and shared vision meant… Kelsey redefined them.

She had read him the letter Page had given her, and one particular section had made him rethink everything.

*Either way, I want to thank you, Kels. Not just for caring for Emma and giving her the life I never could, but for giving me the only friend I ever had. The past three years have been some of the most cathartic, joy and hope filled of my life. Share that joy with my daughter...our daughter...every day of her life.*

At the least, Kelsey would co-parent with him because Page had asked her to. But he didn't want the least. He'd come through so much to be here for his daughter, and he'd assumed that would be enough. It was, but he wanted...*more*. More love, more adventure, more joy. More of what Kelsey brought to both their lives.

But, like being a good dad, showing up for her in a meaningful way would take learning about her, which he wasn't genetically predisposed to do. Would she be patient with him?

"Hey, there, sweetie!" he heard Kelsey exclaim in the other room. "Look up here, Em! Look how big you are, standing all by yourself!"

He smiled. Page had asked for Emma's life to be filled with joy and it was, thanks to Kelsey. God, all he wanted was to give that back to her in spades.

He filled and sucked down another glass of water.

*You can. You already know what she wants to do, and you have the power to make it happen.*

He did, didn't he? He could make her dream of opening more charity centers come true and go from there. If she wanted to talk more about it, they could talk while he put the plans in motion, but he didn't want to sleep on it and lose this opportunity.

He knew good people—people she'd feel comfortable with—but they'd need time to consider it and make shifts to their schedules. Two were in Minnesota—Patrick and Emilia O'Hara—and Patience Rhys ran an obstetrics program in Austin. He'd be doing it for Kelsey, but it would honor Page.

A small tug of hope pulled at his chest as he pictured a sign reading *Page Everson Clinic*.

"You up for adding some pancakes to my order?" Kelsey asked, coming into the room still clad only in his flannel shirt.

His thoughts were wholly interrupted by the sultry sight in front of him. The shirt went down to the top of her thighs, leaving the bottom of her backside on view for his pleasure. Everything about her seemed designed for his pleasure now that he thought about it.

The long, silky curls that he'd run between his fingers had calmed his rapidly beating heart after the sight of her had sent it wild. The soft fingertips that had slid along his back had brought him back to life—especially the part of him that had thoroughly enjoyed Kelsey last night.

She was so much more than he'd given her credit for, and still he wasn't sure what to do with that—except protect it in the same way he strove to protect Emma.

"I could eat, yeah. Did Emma finish her bottle already?"

"Yep, thank goodness. I'm starved. I didn't…
uh…get much time for food last night."

Liam chuckled. "Yeah, I sort of forgot to feed
you, didn't I?"

She reached up on her toes and pressed her lips
to his. "Oh, I ate… But I could do with some other
sustenance now. I think at this point my body could
claim I've violated the Hippocratic oath and am ac-
tively doing it harm by withholding food."

Liam let the woman in his arms kiss him, run
her fingers along his shoulders and biceps, and gen-
erally make him feel as if this was where he was
meant to be.

"Okay. Let's get these pancakes made. Where
do I find the mix?"

She bit her bottom lip and anything halfway
about his erection went all out. Damn, she was
beautiful. How Dex ever let her go was beyond
Liam's comprehension.

"It's at the main house. I'll get dressed and go
grab it," she said.

"Not a chance I'm letting you put clothes on that
magnificent body. Is it in the kitchen pantry?"

She nodded. "Yep. With the cereal. Can you grab
the syrup, too?"

He pointed to his lips. "For a price, I can."

She giggled and met his mouth with hers, open
and hot with passion. Finally she pulled away, and
any clarity he'd needed was there, in the space between their bodies. He cared so much about her and

he wanted to start showing her in ways other than his ardent appreciation of her body.

She sashayed across the kitchen, her taut skin begging to be touched.

*Tomorrow.*

He'd start working on other ways of showing her tomorrow.

"Okay. I'm going," he said. "But only because I know I can get there faster…which means I can cook and then we can get back to what we were up to quicker."

"Oh, here's your phone. I saved the video of Emma and sent it to myself. I hope you don't mind?"

"Of course not."

"You got a few texts while I was filming, but I just swiped out of them. I'll start warming up the pan," she said.

Just like it had in Emma's room, the weight of the phone in his hands was heavy and intrusive. He didn't want to deal with his dad's sudden appearance back in his life. Especially when he knew his old man's pattern—slide in, hang around just long enough to make everyone think he cared, Liam included, before ghosting them.

Liam would *not* let that happen with Kelsey and Emma.

"Thanks. I'll be back in a sec."

He threw on shoes and a shirt and jogged out of the cottage. Instantly the distance between him and the life he was certain he wanted hit him like an RPG, throwing him off kilter.

He paused and opened up his messages. Sure enough, he had three from his dad.

I know you may not believe this, son, but I'd like a chance to get to know her. Before it's too late.

Emma? And too late for what?

The next one wasn't any better.

Please don't ignore me. I know I wasn't the father of the year, but it's not too late to try, is it? I'd like to do that—try—before I'm out of time.

For crying out loud, it was four in the morning. Too early and too late for veiled threats.

The third text finally laid it all out.

I'd like to set up a time for you to come visit so I can talk through your place here at Everson. Please call me back.

*Please?* When had his dad ever *asked* for anything?

Liam looked behind him at the image of Kelsey in his home, dancing around the kitchen in his shirt. His dad was right on one count. It wasn't too late to try. But as for a place at Everson? He *had* a place, and it was here with Kelsey and Emma. God, why did his dad always know how to pull the rug from under him just as he was standing on solid ground?

He shot back a reply:

If you want to see us, you can come here.

The three blinking dots came right away, but disappeared quickly. When they came for thirty straight seconds, Liam held his breath.

The response sent chills racing down his skin, and despite the warm breeze he couldn't stop shaking.

I'm sick, son. Pancreatic cancer, stage three. I wouldn't ask if I didn't think it might be the last time I see you. I'd really like to meet her. Your daughter.

A tear slipped down Liam's cheek.

If this was true, was he being selfish, missing the last months of his dad's life to focus on himself, or had he earned that right?

I'm sorry to hear that. Call me after eleven and we can make a plan.

Liam sighed, conflict brewing in his heart. He might have escaped one prison relatively unscathed, but he still felt as trapped as ever.

# CHAPTER ELEVEN

KELSEY AWOKE TANGLED in sheets, the sun slicing through the slits in the blinds. She twisted her back, which cracked twice, then stretched her neck. God, why was she so sore? Her body shifted and moaned in places she'd only been vaguely aware existed in her anatomy.

When she propped herself up on a raw elbow and saw the disarray of the bedroom, the evening before came back to her in flashes.

The gorgeous room Liam had created for Emma.

Kissing Liam and tasting coffee and cinnamon on her tongue.

Liam's hands roving over her body, bringing every one of her cells back to life.

Making a middle-of-the-night breakfast, then more love, before passing out again.

Heat rose in her cheeks and spread down her chest as she recalled all the ways he'd loved her, touched her, and—oh, my goodness—how she'd touched and loved him in return. It had been a night of give and take and it had been perfect.

As if thinking of the man had conjured him, Liam rounded the corner looking the same way she'd found him the evening before. Shirtless. Ripped. Every muscle one of those she'd enjoyed the night before. The human body had always amazed her, but his…? Well, it brought out her awe in very visceral ways. And he was holding Emma, whom he'd called *"our daughter."*

"Good morning," he said.

He put Emma on the bed in between them and tucked a strand of hair behind Kelsey's ear. The infant giggled and grabbed the sheet, pulling it over her face. She completed the scene that was melting Kelsey's resolve to keep Liam at arm's length.

*I could get used to this.*

"You, too. How long have you been up?"

"About twenty-four hours now."

She gasped but he laughed it off. "Don't worry; I'm more rested now than I have been in…" he checked the spot on his wrist where a watch should be "…two years or so."

Her skin flashed with heat again. "Me, too."

"That was a helluva first date," he said.

He smelled like mint shampoo, and the scent wrapped its way around her good sense, obliterating it.

"So it was a date, then? I was wondering what to call it."

"Of course it was."

Kelsey grinned. Her cheeks were the only part of her body that wasn't sore. "I thought dinner and a movie was the traditional way to go, but I gotta say I like this better."

"I'll agree with you there."

He kissed her and her stomach turned squishy.

It didn't do that at the sight of blood or exposed bone…but a handsome man's lips? Yep.

*Way to go, biology.*

"Thank you for…um…being flexible last night—metaphorically speaking," he said. "I'm sorry I waylaid our dinner plans."

"We can reschedule. Do you have plans this morning?"

"I've got a shift till six."

"I've got a C-section at seven, but how about we see how we feel after that?"

"Wow. This is what two working parents get, huh? But I'd love to see you after work. I'd like to talk about this."

Her pulse sped up as he gestured between the three of them like he had the day they met. "This" had an altogether different connotation, though, and her mind reeled at everything that had changed in barely over a month.

"Me, too. Hey, I was meaning to ask you if everything's all right."

He leaned in and brushed his lips softly against hers, and just like that the squishiness came back.

"Never better. Why do you ask?"

"Oh, just the texts you got last night. They seemed urgent and it was the middle of the night. Just thought I'd make sure you were doing okay."

A storm flashed across his features, turning his eyes a volatile shade of brown instead of the tranquil gold chestnut they usually were.

"I'm fine. Just family stuff."

Family stuff? His father? She wanted to ask him, especially since she considered him part of her family now, but he wouldn't meet her gaze.

"Hey, do you mind if we chat later?" he asked. "I've got to get in for an early-morning meeting."

"Sure. I'll see you in there?"

He smiled, but didn't reply before he shut the bathroom door behind him.

The intentional way he'd circumvented her question sent a shiver of worry through her. She was opening a space for him in her heart and her life, and while he'd seemed game for that the night before, now that had changed.

*Something* had changed.

If she had to choose between good sex—no, *great* sex—and openness and honesty, she'd choose the latter.

At least, she hoped she would.

Kelsey's hands shook as she gathered her clothes, which looked like they'd been torn apart by a grenade. Her scrub pants were on the floor, her shirt on the bed, and her panties had somehow become tied around the bedpost. When she recalled why, every inch of her skin burst into flames.

Liam had been so open with her up until now. *Maybe he regrets it?*

Maybe. But then why did he keep kissing her? Why had he let it happen three times? *No, four!*

Kelsey put Emma in a front-pack and the pair

made their way across the property to the main house. For the first time since purchasing it, four years ago, she didn't feel anything other than indifference as they walked into the foyer. Somehow the cabin, with its cozy decor and now fond memories, felt more like home.

But as she put Emma on her play pad by the sliding glass door Kelsey's chest heaved. It was *Liam*. Liam felt familiar…like home. If home were a person. And that was, oh, so problematic, for all the reasons being attracted to him had been a bad idea yesterday. This, though? This was infinitely worse.

Because she liked him. A lot. Maybe more than liked him. Was it…*love*?

This confusion was exactly why she'd avoided Liam in the first place. She needed to concentrate on the Foundation dinner and her daughter—not moon over a man who might or might not feel the same about her. A man who might or might not leave and go back to a job in Texas at some point. *Ugh.*

She threw her head into a pillow and groaned. Emma giggled and put her blanket back over her own head.

"Hey there, little one," Kelsey cooed. "Looks like it's just you and me again. What do you say we get in our comfiest pajamas and curl up in bed tonight, so we can pretend we *didn't* just meet the best guy in the world that we can't have?"

Emma smacked a tennis-ball-sized red button

on her play table. It rang out with a kids' song that drove Kelsey nuts. Emma loved it, though, so… Well, Kelsey did, too.

When Emma grabbed Kelsey's shirt, and pulled it in to put in her mouth, like she did everything these days, Kelsey cringed.

Of *course* she would walk out of Liam's house with yet another article of his clothing. And of *course* it absolutely reeked of his irresistible scent.

*It's like you're trying to torture yourself with his presence.*

No matter. She'd shower him off, throw the shirt in the laundry, and hope she could erase the feeling of his body pressed against hers just as easily.

She showered, drove off, and dropped Emma at daycare.

Barb gave her the once-over, a smug smile on her face. "You look a little flushed. You okay?"

That was her cue to hightail it out of there before she had to explain that the heat on her cheeks came from certain nocturnal activities with a certain surgeon she should absolutely be avoiding.

*Good grief.*

What had she thought would happen? That they'd end up happily ever after? A bizarre family brought together by pain and loss?

*Yes. That's exactly what you hoped.*

Kelsey bit her lip in frustration. Maybe she had, just a little. And worse…? She still sort of did.

But if this thing they were doing didn't work

out, and Liam asked for custody of Emma, Kelsey would miss so many moments in her daughter's life. Therefore, Liam had to take a back seat in her thoughts.

At least that was the plan. When she walked into the hospital and saw him dip into Kris's office her pulse went wild. It was the look on his face—concern mixed with a determination that was etched around his eyes—that had Kelsey waiting outside instead of heading to her own office to get a jumpstart on her emails.

She told herself she needed to chat with Kris about the Gold Fleece Foundation dinner. But the hushed voices inside had Kelsey moving closer to the slightly ajar door. She tried to focus, but only caught snippets.

"Does she know you're here?" Kris asked, barely audible.

*She?* Herself? Kelsey?

More muffled conversation, then, "It's the right thing to do, Kris."

"I agree."

There was some shuffling of papers, the opening of file cabinet drawers, and then Kris asked, "That sound fair?"

Something unintelligible from Liam.

"Okay, then. It's done. Are you going to say anything?"

"Not yet. I'll wait for a good time."

More veiled discussion she missed.

*Speak up!* she wanted to shout.

Kelsey's imagination was going wild. *What* was done? Was Liam considering quitting, two weeks into his new job? And, from the sounds of it, wasn't going to say anything to her?

A nurse walked by and shot Kelsey a withering stare. Kelsey shrugged. Eavesdropping outside the CMO's office wasn't exactly to be encouraged, but in these circumstances it couldn't be helped.

"Move along. Nothing to see here," she muttered as the pink-scrubs-clad nurse headed to Pediatrics.

It *was* rather ridiculous, just waiting to hear snippets of information from behind an oak door. Kelsey steeled herself. Only one way to find out. She knocked on the door.

"Just a second," Kris called out. Then, "Are we good here?"

"We are. And thanks for your discretion."

"Of course," Kris said in a low voice, before switching back to call, "Come on in!"

Kelsey walked in, a smile on her face. Until she looked at Liam. His gaze met hers, and while the familiar warmth was there, so was something else. It felt like a wall had been erected.

Heat rose up his neck in splashes of red and she felt her own skin warming as well. Well, that was inconvenient. She hadn't really considered what making love and then seeing each other at work would be like. Awkward, apparently. Still, he gave no other indication that anything was wrong.

"Hey, Kelsey. I was just talking to Kris about how nice it's been working with you."

Kelsey's gaze sharpened. "Oh, yeah? Well, we had a good save yesterday, so I'd have to agree there."

Except that was *not* what she'd heard his hushed voice discussing with their boss. Or maybe it was just *her* boss now.

"I saw the report, Kelsey. It was a good save indeed. Which makes me think…have you considered asking Liam for help with the Gold Fleece dinner? You two work well together. I'm sorry I'm only just now thinking of it. I've been meaning to ask you how the planning is going, but with Dexter coming back and the board breathing down my neck about the fallout from the whole Emma Hartley disaster… She's a fabulous actress, but good grief, was she bad press for the hospital at first. You know we just got back to our patient care goal from before Owen tried to help fix her botched surgery?"

"Wow. That's wild. But, yeah… It's no problem. Liam's got plenty on his plate without my—"

"No," Liam said, interrupting her. "I'd love to help. Why don't we talk about it at lunch? Noon in the cafeteria?"

Kelsey swallowed back the lump that had gotten lodged in her throat. She considered telling him she was too busy, but they'd talked about their schedules that morning.

"Um…sure. Noon is…noon is good."

"There. It's settled. Anything else you came in for, Kelsey? I have a meeting I have to get to, but you can swing by this afternoon if you'd like."

Kris all but pushed them out into the hallway, where the silence wrapped around Kelsey like a blanket. Kelsey shook her head, trying to clear her swirling thoughts over what had just happened.

Why would Kris push Liam onto her project if he was leaving?

"Sorry if I was gruff earlier this morning. I just needed some coffee," Liam said.

"It's fine. Everything okay with you and Kris?"

She watched his face for clues, but the stubborn man didn't give so much as an errant blink to let her know what he was thinking.

"Yep. Great. She was just checking in…seeing how things are going."

*Not true.*

Her stomach sank. As it turned out, there *was* something just as awful as people she loved getting hurt. Being lied to felt like someone scraping at an open wound.

*How had she let herself sleep with him?*

"You don't need to take on the Foundation dinner planning with me. It's pretty straightforward and I've got it handled."

"I meant it, Kelsey. We make a good team. Besides, I can't wait to see what you do with the Foundation."

Kelsey didn't disagree with him. But team members talked to each other—and in the past couple of hours that had shifted.

"Okay, well…thanks, then."

"And maybe we can give some more thought to the satellite centers?"

"I don't know… If I went with that option, I'd lose so much control over how the charity is run and who's in charge. I'm not sure I'm comfortable with that."

"But wouldn't you serve more families?"

"Maybe… Yes. But there's the potential for more loss—less stringent protocols. It might not be worth it."

"Hmm… I'm not sure I agree. Would you be open to me sharing some ideas at lunch?"

His hand rested on her arm and heat blossomed from the area. He bent down, his lips pursed, like he meant to kiss her. and she froze before leaning backwards.

"Um… Liam, I don't think we should—"

She stumbled, and would have toppled to the ground if steady hands hadn't caught her.

"Whoa, there. We're in a hospital, but I still wouldn't advise taking unnecessary spills!"

*No, no, please no.*

She knew that voice, and even though it no longer had a hold on her, she didn't want to come face to face with its owner for the first time since their breakup while avoiding kissing the man she'd just slept with.

"Nice catch, Dex," Liam said, reaching out to shake Dexter's hand as he steadied Kelsey.

"Thanks. You settling in okay?" Dex asked, avoiding Kelsey's gaze.

His hair had grown out, even grayed along the temples, but otherwise he was just as handsome as the day he'd walked out on her. But, strangely, she didn't feel a thing looking at him.

Liam, on the other hand…

"I am—thanks to this one, here."

"Kelsey, yes… It's good to see you."

"You, too," she said, her voice as firm and unemotional as she could make it.

"Anyway," Dex said, his focus back on Liam, "I was thinking about you the other day, when I signed up for a trauma conference outside Seattle. That guy I told you about—the one who works with PTSD and patients who have lost their spouses—he'll be there. Want me to send you the link?"

"That sounds great, thanks. He sounds like the real deal."

*Wait.* Liam and Dexter had *talked*? About things that *mattered*?

Her world tipped off its axis, sending her spinning.

"Are you headed to see Kris?" she asked Dex.

"Yeah, I'm helping her and Owen plan for the big day."

*Oh, yeah.* She'd conveniently forgotten that just before heading to Africa, Owen Rhys, their Chief of Plastics, had proposed to the boss and she'd said yes. It had been a scandal at first, but now Kelsey found it adorable.

"The big day?" Liam asked.

"Yeah. I'm late, so Kels can explain. But Liam, give me a call if you want to grab a beer sometime."

"You bet."

Dex jogged down to Kris's door and opened it without knocking. Kelsey really, truly didn't feel a thing for the man, but that didn't mean his dismissal of her didn't sting. They'd spent *two years* together.

Liam spoke. "Is this the first time you've talked to him since...?"

She nodded.

"Ouch. I'm sorry. And I'm sorry if it seemed like I'm chummy with the guy. I'm not, but he's been helpful in getting me situated when you're not here."

"It's fine."

His brows touched together with concern.

"Really, it is."

"Hey..." he said, rubbing her arms.

It soothed her at the same time it sent flames racing over her skin.

"I'm here to talk."

Talk? She'd love to. But only if he would share something—*anything*—about what he was keeping from her. Until then, what could she say that wouldn't shine a spotlight on her vulnerability while shrouding Liam's in shadow? Between the middle-of-the-night texts he'd brushed off to this secret meeting with Kris, Kelsey was in the dark.

"Thanks. I've just got a lot on my mind right now."

"Okay…well, the offer stands."

"I appreciate it. However, we've got the Gold Fleece Foundation dinner to plan and a child to take care of while we both navigate pretty full-time gigs. Why don't we just put what happened last night on the back burner for now?"

His gaze held hers for longer than was comfortable. "Are you sure?" he asked.

She hesitated for long enough to see the hope reach his eyes. But finally, she nodded.

"I am. I like you, Liam. A lot. And you're an incredible father and surgeon. Focus on those right now and I'll do the same. We owe it to Emma."

The hope fizzled out and she almost caved and took it all back.

"If that's what you want, then I'll support it," he said. "But I like you too, Kelsey, and I'd like to see where this could go." He sighed. "I'll see you at lunch?"

"Okay." He liked her? Then why the secrecy? "Thanks for taking on the Foundation dinner, Liam."

"Of course. I'm always here, Kelsey. For anything you need."

Those last words were ripe with meaning and

emotion. But she wasn't sure how to decipher them anymore.

As she turned back down the hall toward her wing of the hospital she let a few rogue tears slip down her cheek. She'd been so full of hopeful optimism a month ago, with a career she loved, a new daughter to cherish, and a future she could look forward to. That alone should have been enough. But then she'd been foolish enough to wish for more and seek it out with a man she knew would throw off the careful balance she'd kept.

And knowing love, passion, and the comfort of a family—even briefly—had changed her. For the briefest of moments she'd even believed, believed she deserved that kind of life, despite stealing it from those she loved most.

Now everything—the job, the family, the love— was slipping from her grasp, and she didn't have a clue what to do about it.

Her day at work didn't help, either. The backlog of patients after the emergency the night before took away any chance she'd had for a break— including her lunch with Liam. He'd understood, but she'd heard the disappointment in his voice.

*One more reason to let him go.*

The C-section went as smoothly as it could have, but the social media cameras in Kelsey's face were something she'd never get used to. Maybe it was time to rethink her practice. Being an OB to Hollywood's finest was lucrative, but not nearly as rewarding as her Gold Fleece work. Which she needed to get started on first thing tomorrow.

What would it be like to take Liam's advice and expand? She'd said it was her dream when the first year of the charity had been so successful, but somewhere along the way she'd stopped meaning it—and she knew exactly where, actually.

*After Page.*

When Kelsey had invited another OB in it had ended in catastrophe, and Kelsey had seen first-hand how it had destroyed a family.

Exhaustion and defeat wore her down as these thoughts and their less fun friends plagued her during the drive home.

She made it back, but from the way her eyelids drooped she wasn't sure she had more energy left than what it would take to brush her teeth and forget this day had ever happened.

Annoyance prickled her skin when she saw the note taped to her front door.

*Come by the cabin when you're home. Please. Let me help you wash today away, maybe explain a few things...and then help you make the Foundation dinner amazing. I promise I'll feed you this time, too...*

She wanted to. It was like he'd read her mind about needing their shared vulnerability back. Every cell in her heart screamed at her to give in, but her mind wouldn't budge. Logic worked against her, reminding her of the canyon of unknowns separating them.

Would he go back to Texas?

Would he want the same things she did—a partner and family—when he'd had that already and lost it?

*Of course, there was sweet Emma to think of, too.*

She could be a bridge spanning the gap or an earthquake widening it.

What was keeping Kelsey from fully giving in where Liam was involved?

Her heart won the fight and, regardless of the consequences, she walked up the path to the cabin, her energy somehow restored. She was a scientist—surely she could compartmentalize her feelings for the man and just enjoy him while they were forced to be together.

She knocked, and didn't have to wait more than half a second for the door to open and showing her all the reasons this had been a good idea. Liam wore a loose-fitting T-shirt and jeans, and somehow pulled them off as much as he had his scrubs and the suit she'd been lucky enough to see him in.

She swallowed back the wave of lust that overrode her ability to make smart choices.

"I'm not staying the night because I think we can both agree my plan to keep this professional is for the best. This is just…for fun," she said, skipping a hello.

Her heart bucked at the idea, and her underwear was already damp with her desire.

He spun her around and into his arms, brushing her bangs out of her eyes like she always tried to do. And then he kissed her. Softly at first, then with an urgency that consumed her.

Okay, maybe his body was enough. For now.

When he pulled away, there wasn't a shred of logic anyone could have flung at her to make her change her mind.

*She liked this man. A lot.*

And she wanted him in her bed. Or his. It really didn't matter as long as he was naked and underneath her.

"I can do fun," he said.

She didn't wait for him to make the move this time, or to finish his thought. She reached up on her toes and took his face in her hands, pulling it down to hers.

Liam's hands cupped her butt, using it as leverage to press their bodies together, and she didn't mind one bit. One of them moaned with pleasure at the intensity of the kiss…or maybe they both did. Either way, it was her who pulled back—and when she did she saw his ideas for her Foundation typed and printed and laid out on the table. There were even photos interspersed between binkies and bottles.

Dammit. How did he always know just the thing to reel her back in?

"Thank you for helping with the Foundation dinner," she whispered against his mouth, punctuating it with a kiss.

It really would be nice to have his insight.

"You're welcome. And before you ask, I'm not doing it to get you in bed again. Not that I'll complain if that's where we end up, but I just… I just want more women to have access to what Page did. And…and I'd like to honor her by helping your Foundation thrive."

Kelsey nodded, her forehead against his chest. "I want that, too."

But somewhere in the month since she'd met Liam, she'd also begun wanting *more*.

"It's inspiring me to look into work I can do to help those who need it," he said.

There he went, reading her mind again.

"Oh, yeah? Care to share?" she asked.

"Not yet."

Her face fell, and he must have noticed.

"But I promise I will. I know the day has been… weird, but I do want to talk to you. Just give me time?"

She nodded and grabbed his hand, pulling him into the cabin. If he wouldn't talk to her now, she would just enjoy *this* part of being neighbors with Liam at least.

"Kelsey, wait," he said as they got inside the door. "This date has protocols that must be followed."

She pretended to frown, but a smile tugged at her lips. "You ER doctors and your protocols. But okay…walk me through the interventions."

He grinned. "Of course, Dr. Gaines. Well, first there's a diagnostic I have to run, to see if we're compatible."

"Oh, yeah? I thought we established that in the last run of physical tests."

She bit back a giggle. She'd only dated one other healthcare professional, and Dex had kept their relationship separate from work on all fronts. This whole ability to speak a shared language and make a sexy game of it was new to her.

*New and provocative as heck.*

Had she really been tired when she'd got home? Even now, she couldn't remember. Also conveniently absent was her self-imposed mandate not to do this again until she and Liam had talked.

"We did, but I need a second opinion."

Liam swept her up in his arms in a single move that had her head spinning and her heart racing.

He placed his cheek to her breast and sighed. "Just as I thought. Elevated pulse. Possible attraction."

She nuzzled against his neck. "There's nothing 'possible' about it, Dr. Everson. I want you."

He set her down gently, but didn't release her.

"I want you, too. But there's one more test we have to run." He bent down and kissed her. At the same time he put his hand over her eyes. "Do you trust me?"

She didn't hesitate in responding, even though her heart clenched with worry. "I do, Liam. I trust you."

She would overthink the red flags pinging in her head tomorrow. Tonight was about the rest of her body.

"Good. Close your eyes and wait here."

She nodded, and when she heard him walk away she bit back a nervous laugh. Where would she go without his steady grasp? Because he'd kissed her to the point of dizziness and, good grief, her mind was spinning with a heady blend of exhaustion and lust.

Sounds of a cello—maybe two?—filled the space, wrapping her in auditory bliss. Her other senses were heightened, too. She inhaled through her nose and smiled. The air was suddenly permeated with a floral aroma.

Liam's arm wrapped around her waist, drawing her back to him. When his lips brushed over the exposed skin on her neck she shuddered with anticipation.

"Dr. Gaines, if you'll be so kind as to follow me?"

Kelsey didn't have a chance to respond before she was whisked up into his arms again. She squealed and held tight to his neck, her eyes still closed.

This time when he set her down it was on his

bed. She recognized the soft give of the down comforter beneath her.

"Keep your eyes shut. If you can pass this test, you'll be a star subject."

"Whatever you say, Doc. I'm at your mercy."

"That's a good patient. Now, lie down."

She did as she was instructed, her back arched in satisfaction. Her fists gripped the comforter for something to ground her as the rest of her body was electrically charged.

His hands trailed down her legs, removing her scrub bottoms in the process. Her skin was on fire, her mouth dry, but her core was molten lava, hot and wet.

Her symptoms worsened as his fingers slid over her hips.

"I think these have to go," he growled. "They've been compromised."

He linked his thumbs along the lace of her underwear and tugged them over her curves. He didn't remove them entirely, though, just left them tight around her ankles as his hands lifted her shirt over her breasts, exposing them. He draped the fabric along her collarbone.

She let out a small cry of delight as his mouth found its way down the center of her body, his hands holding her arms in place by her sides. She was trapped as tightly as if she was in the MRI lab, but it wasn't claustrophobic in the least. If anything, it was freeing, following Liam's commands and being the center of his focused attention.

*Freeing...and hot as sin.*

"You're doing well, Dr. Gaines. We're almost at the end and you've been very patient. I think you deserve a small reward for being so...open."

He finally slipped her underwear from her ankles and spread her legs so she was completely bared for him. Her soft cries grew in intensity as his mouth, his hands, his tongue, all worked in unison to bring her to climax. It didn't take long, but it was the most intense form of pleasure she'd ever experienced. She hugged him close when she'd calmed down enough to regain any strength in her arms and he put her head on his chest, playing with her hair until her breathing slowed.

"You can open your eyes now," he whispered, trailing a finger along her stomach.

Breathless, she opened her eyes, expecting to be inundated with the harsh overhead lights, breaking the spell he'd put her under.

Instead, she was met with an adult version of what Liam had done for Emma the other day. The room was lit exclusively with candles of every shape and size and decorated with plumeria—she'd missed that scent somehow—and roses. Framed beside his bed was a photo of her holding Emma above her head, both of them caught mid-laugh, the ocean sparking in the background.

When had he taken that?

The gesture warmed her heart but confused it as well.

What did it mean?

"It's beautiful, Liam. How did you know about the plumeria?"

She'd told him her favorite flowers were roses when he'd asked, but her love of the tropical flower was a secret she'd held tight in her chest since she was a preteen.

"Mike. He's a wealth of information about you. I'd be worried if he was ever held captive for state secrets. One promise of tamales from Texas and he gave up everything."

They shared a laugh and then Kelsey gazed up at Liam, her body tired and her mind finally silent. "What's the occasion?"

"Just me wanting to show you how much you mean to me… I know there's a lot behind and between us, but I care about you, Kelsey. I have since I first saw you in those grungy old gray sweatpants."

She laughed, remembering the time he'd come by the house unannounced to take Emma for a walk in the sand and she'd answered the door in stained sweats, with her hair ratty enough to house a flock of sparrows. "I burned them right after you left."

"Damn. I was hoping to do a bit of frustrated-mommy-meets-single-pediatrician role-playing later."

He winked, kicking up her pulse like that little move always did.

"Oh, I think I can dredge something up for that. I do have one question, though. You aren't taking any new patients, are you?"

The eruption of laughter that he let loose was infectious. He kissed her forehead and squeezed her tighter against his still-clothed chest.

"No. Absolutely not. It's just you, sweetheart. I think you'll be more than enough to keep my practice thriving."

It was her turn to laugh as hope took flight in her chest again. Maybe if she just lay back and enjoyed the man, without making a federal case out of everything he did or didn't say, this would be okay.

More than okay, actually...

He made her come twice more, then lay next to her sated and replete body.

"What's that?" she asked, pointing to a small suitcase with a cartoon dinosaur on the front.

Liam tensed, but his smile stayed glued in place.

"I was hoping to chat about that after dinner, actually," he said, jumping up to grab it. "It's—" he started, but a crashing of glass and metal that sounded as if it was just outside the front door, interrupted him.

Kelsey shot out of bed, tugging her shirt down and pulling on her scrubs. "What was that?" she asked.

Her teeth chattered and she was suddenly cold. Probably from the twelve hours she'd been on shift.

Liam had gone still, every muscle on edge, his gaze sharpened. "A car crash."

In a rush, she realized his stance was that of an Army-trained trauma surgeon. Ready, confident, experienced.

He went to a drawer and pulled out a bright yellow sweatshirt with reflective tape along the side. "Put this on. That came from the road by the driveway, and from the sound of it they hit a tree. We've got to hurry, Kelsey."

"I'm going to call my dad and let him know what's going on."

"Tell him to bring some lights—anything to warn other vehicles coming around that bend that we're there. Then call Mercy and warn them we'll soon be en route."

She nodded and made the calls. Her dad was changing Emma's diaper and putting her back to bed, but would meet them in less than five minutes with the baby monitor in hand.

Liam grabbed the comforter and some towels from the bathroom, then went back for a bottle of hand sanitizer and the bandages he kept in the medicine cabinet.

*God...they might not be enough.*

Liam nodded at her to follow him and tore out of the cabin.

Her heart raced and her legs trembled as they ran out to the road.

*Oh, God.*

It was so much worse than anything she could have imagined.

# CHAPTER TWELVE

LIAM SURVEYED THE SCENE, categorizing the triage.

One-car collision, skid marks indicating that the driver had slowed before plowing into a sixty-foot oak tree. Glass and debris everywhere.

There appeared to be only two passengers inside the vehicle. One male, one female. Liam jogged around the back of the car, and even with the limited light from the cabin's back porch, he could tell no one else was inside. All four windows were shattered, but a web of broken glass was still inside the frame of the windshield. Which meant no one had been thrown from the vehicle. Right now, that was a good thing.

"Oh, my God," Kelsey whispered.

He followed her gaze and saw the head wound on the driver, who was awake but disoriented. There was a thick line of blood pouring from a gaping but clean-looking wound. More concerning was the potential for brain trauma.

He ran over to the driver's side and tried to wrench open the door, but it was dented and stuck. Nothing but the jaws of life would get through. He'd have to go in from the passenger side.

"I'm dialing 911."

"Tell them it's a two person, one-car collision. Driver's side door sealed shut. No victims thrown from the vehicle. Male victim conscious but unresponsive. Female victim unconscious but breathing. And Kels?"

"Yeah?"

"I'm glad you're here. We've got this."

"We do."

Her hands shook, but he didn't worry; he believed in her.

He sprinted to the passenger side and opened the door easily.

"Dammit," he cursed, when he saw the woman, slumped over and barely conscious. He assessed her other injuries and when he felt it was safe, called out: "Kels!" he yelled, tucking his arm under the woman's neck, the other under her knees and as carefully as he could pulling her from the car. "I need you over here."

She ran over, and her face went white when she looked down at the woman in his arms.

"Do you have them on the line?" he asked.

"Not yet. Did her water break?"

He nodded.

"Okay, I'll lay a blanket out. If she's in active labor we need to start helping her transition."

"I agree. Tell the EMTs to hurry."

Kelsey passed on the instructions to the dispatcher and laid the phone beside them on speaker. The EMTs wanted the line to remain open in case there was any issue getting to them.

"You have control, here—okay, Kels? I'm gonna help the guy."

"Got it," Kelsey said.

Kelsey found the bottle of hand sanitizer and covered her hands. The woman had opened her eyes and her low moans had turned to screams.

"We were heading to Mercy…" the mother whispered, clutching her swollen belly. "I'm having a baby." She squeezed Kelsey's hand.

"Do you need anything for your patient before I go?" asked Liam.

He was in awe at Kelsey's confidence. This exam room might be different, and her patient had escalated to crisis mode quicker than usual, but Kelsey had control.

"I'm good. The EMTs will be here soon."

Mike showed up and, like his daughter, who was already assisting the patient through early labor, got to work without saying any more than, "Emma's safe in bed. I've got eyes on her with the monitor but I'll run back if she wakes up."

He set up cones and floodlights while Kelsey took vitals. Liam instructed Mike to go and guide the EMTs down the driveway.

They were in their element.

Liam couldn't focus on Kelsey or her patient—not when he was extracting the driver from the car over the center console and treating his head laceration after making sure it was safe to move him. However, out of the corner of his vision he saw Kelsey at work and awe surged through him.

*She's incredible. The perfect partner.*

They paced each other, calling out stats and working fast, but not frantically. It was a dance, with both of them keeping step and time like they'd always worked together on roadside trauma.

Liam cleaned his patient's wound, checked his pupils, then rechecked his pulse.

Kelsey set up a workstation, complete with a makeshift bed made of towels and blankets.

Liam bandaged the man's head and checked his body for any bruising that would indicate internal bleeds he'd want the ER to know about.

Kelsey propped up her patient's knees and checked her cervix.

Liam cut off the man's belt and shirt, so the EMTs could work on his chest, where a blue-gray discoloration had started to spread from the center.

Kelsey talked her patient through the steps she was taking and asked what the baby's name was going to be.

Liam could tell the new mother was already calming down under Kelsey's expert care.

The woman screamed through a contraction just at the same time as the ambulance wailed its oncoming approach. Mike guided it into the top of the drive, and as they exited filled in the EMTs on what the two doctors were up to.

"The pregnant female's midway through delivery, and that fellow over there has had a wound about four inches long, deep enough to see bone, cleaned and bandaged. This guy is a trauma surgeon and she's an OB, so both victims are in good hands."

"I'm getting in the rig with her," Kelsey called out as they moved her patient to a spinal board and strapped her in, in a way that would allow Kelsey to guide her through the birth in transit, if necessary.

It wasn't how the mother had probably imagined bringing her infant into the world, but if everyone made it through unscathed it would be a heck of a story.

"I'll be right behind you with my guy," said Liam, and gratefulness surged in his chest for Mike and Kelsey.

Seeing the crashed car, the blood, smelling the scent of burnt rubber and smoke permeating his clothes—all of it had brought him back to a place where he'd barely survived. It probably always would. But his captivity no longer held his mind hostage; it was a part of him he'd learned to work around. Now shoved it back where it belonged, into the recesses of his mind, and concentrated on Kelsey, who was speeding off with her patient.

She, Mike, and Emma were his mooring—his tether to the reality outside this event.

*If your father doesn't make that list, why are you leaving to see him?*

"No. Not right now," Liam said aloud, shutting off his overactive subconscious.

The EMTs joined Liam in assessing the now-unconscious male victim—Peter, his wife had told

Kelsey. They loaded him on a stretcher and put him in the vehicle, and were still hooking him up to IVs and monitors as they slammed the doors and drove to Mercy.

When they got to the ER, Liam jumped out and met the attending on call. He shared the patient's vitals and threw on a gown while he talked.

"Hey, Dr. Howard," he said to the trauma surgeon on call. "Want my help?"

"Yep. Miller called in sick. Get the patient set up in a trauma room. I want a CT of his head and abdomen, stat."

Something caught Liam's eye in the corner of the parking lot. "Be right there."

Liam jogged over to where Kelsey was squatting on the ground. Her arms were wrapped tight around her knees and the look on her face was somber. He dropped beside her and draped his body over hers like a weighted blanket.

"You okay?"

She nodded, but didn't reply.

"That was intense. Look at me, Kels."

Her eyes met his and he recognized the fear in them. She needed to be in control. He understood what losing Page and her mother had done to shape that side of her.

"How is the mother?" he asked.

"She had the baby. A little girl. It could've gone the other way, but they'll…they'll be okay," she said, glancing at him. "I've never trusted anyone to work with me before, but you…you were incredible."

"You did amazing, too, Kels. That baby girl was lucky she found your oak tree and you could bring her into the world."

Kelsey's eyes grew wide and she gasped.

"Sorry…sorry!" Liam said. "That would be my ill-timed military humor. I'm so sorry."

He pulled her onto his lap, wrapped her in his arms, and held her as a flood of emotions broke through her carefully constructed wall. All he wanted was to comfort her, make sure she knew she was safe. And his job wasn't done yet.

"I've never done anything like that before," she said.

"I know, but you did great. You were a pro, and that mother and baby are alive because of you."

Kelsey's tears picked up again, but her pulse was normal and her eyes had lost their anxiety. Liam buried his face in Kelsey's hair, breathing in the scent of plumeria she carried with her.

Kelsey nodded. "I was so scared…so absolutely terrified that I'd…"

"But you didn't. She's fine. Come on. Let's go sit down inside. You need some hot tea. And when I'm done saving the other patient, I'm curling up with you for the rest of the night, okay?"

"Yes, please. Someday I hope I can be as calm and measured as you after an emergency save like we just had."

Liam considered what she'd said.

He knew what it took to get to a place where he could look at a man bleeding out on the street and think that it wasn't even in the top ten of the worst things he'd seen. The truth was, he *wasn't* calm and measured; he was broken and patched back together.

Her turning out like him was the last thing he wanted.

He got Kelsey settled and ran back to Trauma One, where his patient was being intubated and given the drugs he'd need to slow the internal bleeding.

"CT's ordered and head lac's clean, but he's losing pressure," the nurse called out.

"Get it back. Give him one of epi."

The nurse did so, but before they could see it take effect the steady beep of the monitor rang loud in the sterile room.

"Damn it, he's crashing. Charge to one-fifty and start compressions."

Liam could *not* lose this patient. Not after the man's wife had just delivered their baby into the world. The guy hadn't even met his child…

Minutes passed and nothing changed.

Liam grasped the paddles in each hand, his eyes focused, his gaze on the monitor. It was supposed to show vital signs, but as of now his patient—a thirty-four-year-old man—didn't have any.

"Charge to two hundred," he instructed.

The nurse working the defibrillator nodded and repeated his command back to him.

"Clear!" Liam called out.

Everyone backed away from the gurney so Liam could shock his patient back to life.

No change to the monitor.

He glanced at his watch.

"Come on," he whispered under his breath.

It had been nineteen minutes of chest compressions and no sinus rhythm. Not necessarily too long, but another minute or two and it would be.

"Don't you dare be my first. I won't allow it."

Liam hadn't lost any patient outside his military tenure yet—and that was saying something, considering the busload of retirees on their way to see the Hollywood sign, who had been hit by a heavy-duty truck driven by a guy on his phone. The whole rig had slid down an embankment and half the passengers had been Mercy patients by that evening. So no way was he letting this guy—who'd been doing something as simple as trying to get his wife to Mercy to deliver their child—die on his table.

Life couldn't be that unfair. No damn way.

"Charge!"

"Dr. Everson," the nurse said, her gaze on the clock above the monitor. "It's been twenty minutes."

"I know. But he's got a new baby upstairs and I want him to meet her. Charge to two hundred," he said.

She nodded, but her face shook with disapproval.

He couldn't worry about that right now. He was the doc in charge. "Clear!"

He shocked the man again and still nothing.

"Charge to three hundred."

"Dr. Everson..." the nurse chastised.

"Okay. Let's wait." He paused, waiting it out, praying for the patient to get a sinus rhythm back.

Nothing. Not a damn thing.

"Dr. Everson, he's gone. You have to call it."

"Yeah," he said, shaking his head and sighing. "Okay. Time of death—one forty-four a.m."

A hand rested on his shoulder. "We need to inform the family."

He nodded. "Of course. I'll take care of it."

He walked up to the birthing suites and felt his knees lock when he saw the man's wife in a delivery bed, rocking her infant in her arms. A smile spread across her face when she recognized Liam, and his heart slammed against his chest.

"How is he?" the wife whispered, sitting up.

When he didn't answer right away, she let out a nervous laugh.

"Peter took that corner too fast. I tried to tell him to slow down, that we had time before I went into active labor, but I didn't get the chance. We...we swerved and hit the tree."

*Peter.*

He vowed never to forget that name. Peter wasn't just a statistic to him—he was a patient...a person who'd left behind an entire world. Every patient was the same—whether they lived or died on Liam's table meant more than just another save or loss. It meant a person got another chance, or they didn't. Someone got to go home to their family, or they didn't.

"I'm so sorry, but your husband didn't make it," Liam said.

"Excuse me?" the woman asked.

Her breathing had shifted, though, so she must have heard him—at least on some level.

*Please don't make me say it again.*

But this wasn't about him. It was about her. And he'd stick around as long as he needed to.

"Peter sustained too much trauma and—"

"No, he can't be gone. He…he can't. He didn't get to meet… What happened?" the woman asked, clutching the child tighter to her chest.

"His internal injuries were too severe. I'm so sorry for your loss."

The keening cry Peter's wife let loose was primal and filled with agony. Though he hadn't been with Page when she'd died, he understood the emotions pouring from this woman. His whole career had been sprinkled with loss—the loss of colleagues and friends in his company, then the death of his own spouse. It was an awful, open pit of grief that had only recently begun to close.

"What will we do without him?"

One of the nurses behind them mentioned Dr.

Gaines. *Kelsey.* His pulse kicked up a notch and he looked in the direction of the birthing suites, all beeping and busy.

If anything ever happened to *her*... God, he'd feel just like Peter's wife—despondent and unsure of how to go on living. She—the steady presence responsible for suturing shut his emotional wounds—mattered that much to him.

He could hear his father's admonition now. *"I told you, Liam. Love is for the weak."*

*But you're not him*, his heart protested. *You have so much love to share.*

Peter's wife sank into the depths of the bed. Her skin was pale and she looked clammy. Kelsey should check on her. She seemed hypertensive... low blood pressure.

As if thinking her name was all he needed to do Kelsey was there, in front of him, standing beside the wife—the *widow*, Liam's brain corrected—dictating orders to a nurse about getting the woman hooked up to monitors.

"I'm here to help you," Kelsey told her patient.

But who would help him? Because his heart was right. He had so much to give—enough to care for two incredible women and not feel torn in half. But only if he fixed the part that had been damaged by years of neglect. For all the therapy he'd undergone to get his head around the trauma of his capture, he still hadn't realized the hurt he carried about his father's dismissal of him.

It wasn't too late. He already had the plane tickets. Now he just needed the courage and the right words to say before he lost the chance for good.

He watched Kelsey talking to Peter's wife and his chest swelled with pride...and something stronger. She was worth repairing the wounds of the past for. After all, it was she who had given him a reason to love again.

"How's she doing?" he asked.

"She's in shock."

"I'm sorry. I tried everything—"

"I know. But..." She lowered her voice. "This isn't appropriate here. Want to meet in my office in a few minutes?"

"Sure."

He made his way to her office, passing by the daycare center on his way. Sun peeked through the blinds on the window and the room was alive with the laughter and cries of infants.

It was morning already. A new day...a new chance to get things right.

He caught sight of a familiar tuft of blonde hair and smiled.

*Emma.*

Mike must have dropped her off on his way to the VA.

Liam's smile fell. By some slim thread of fate working in his favor he'd been able to meet that precious little girl in there. Peter wouldn't ever get that chance, and that made Liam feel worse.

Emma was his greatest achievement, and he'd used her as an excuse. An excuse not to connect with his father, not to face his childhood, to keep Kelsey at arm's length about all of that. But he wanted to share his life with her—which meant learning how to share the scary stuff, not just the good parts of his life.

For the woman who'd helped him grow into a father for Emma he could do it.

*I'm sorry, Em. But I'll make it right so hopefully we can all be a family. For good.*

Seconds passed—minutes?—and he found himself in Kelsey's office. He flexed his fingers, shaking out his hands. He cracked his neck, the sound loud in his ears. Nerves fluttered like moths in his chest. What he needed to tell her would have been so much easier in the comfort of the cabin, nestled in each other's arms.

He was going to Austin to forgive his father.

When she walked in, he stood to greet her.

God, she was beautiful. No way was it healthy to feel the way he did about her in such a short amount of time. But staring at her now, her hair tied up in a loose ponytail, her scrubs hiding curves he knew by heart, he realized that tonight had proved one thing—he really cared about this woman. She was making this brave move of his possible.

"Hey, Kels."

"How are you feeling?" she asked.

*Like I could fly. Tell me you feel the way I do about you and I will.*

But she meant about losing his patient.

"I'm okay. I feel horrible for Peter's wife, but there was nothing more we could do. I'm just grateful she's alive to love that little girl. I can't imagine what it would have been like for Emma never to have known either Page or I."

"I'm so sorry." Kelsey was at his side in two steps and she wrapped his hand in both of hers. "But I understand. I thought the same thing—that at least that little girl will have her mother to share Peter with her. Like Emma has you."

"Can we talk?" he asked.

"Sure. Here or at home?"

"Here, I think. I'm a little worried that if I go back to the cabin with you I'll be tempted to do that thing we're so good at that doesn't involve much talking."

She smiled. "We *are* pretty good at that, aren't we?"

"We are—and that's why I need you to sit over there and me to stay here, so I can get this out. It's important. I thought I'd be able to do this over dinner, but it seems like you and I are destined to have any meal we try to have together thwarted."

He chuckled, but her gaze was focused, worry lines appearing along her eyes.

She walked over to the chair behind her desk and sat. "Liam, you're scaring me."

"I'm sorry; that's the last thing I want. In fact, I don't want to hurt you ever again."

"Is this why you won't talk to me? Because you're trying to let me down easy?"

"I'll talk to you, Kels. About anything. And I'm not trying to let you down at all. What do you want to know? I'll tell you."

She didn't hesitate. "I want to know what your greatest fear is."

He sat back in the plush office chair, stunned. That was the last thing he'd expected her to ask.

"Becoming my father. Or, I guess, any of the myriad iterations of that. Letting Emma down... not being there when she needs me most...putting my dreams and desires ahead of hers and having her resent me."

"Do you want to know what I thought when I met you?" she asked.

His gaze narrowed. "Do I...?"

She smirked. "I thought you were a new dad with a ton of stuff to learn, but that you wouldn't stop until you did. I knew right away you were going to be an amazing father—and guess what?"

"What?"

"I was right. You show up for Emma in a thousand ways I never even thought of, and to be honest, when I see you two together, I'm a little jealous."

Liam's heart sounded like he had a stethoscope on it…it was so loud in his ears.

"Thank you. But you don't have anything to be jealous of. Emma loves you. Her face looks like the baby version of someone bringing ice cream when you walk in the room."

"I guess we're doing okay, then? As parents?"

"Yeah, I'd say we are," he replied.

"So, I'll ask you again—what're you so worried about?"

His smile was instant. "Touché."

She shrugged and sent him a wink.

He laughed. "Did you just use my trademark move against me?"

She shrugged again, and his laugh turned into a full-bodied chest rumble.

"Kelsey Gaines, you're as rare and spectacular as a medical board meeting that's canceled and sent as an email instead."

"Wow. No wonder you want out of this. I sound as boring as a post-op write-up for a fistula."

"Who says I want out?"

Kelsey's smile fell, but her gaze lingered on Liam's. "You weren't talking to Kris about your work here so far. And those texts that came in the middle of the night weren't benign. I don't need to know what it's all about, but when I asked, and you lied, it seemed pretty obvious how you felt about me. You only needed to tell me it wasn't any of my business."

"Kels… I know how that must look, and I'm sorry. I just wanted to wait until I had plans made in case I chickened out."

She tilted her head, as if trying to figure out the meaning behind his words.

"I'm going back to Austin to see my dad. You told me to forgive him, and over the past month you've given me the courage to try."

"Wow, Liam. That's great. How long are you going back for?"

"A couple days."

"I'm glad you're going, but we'll miss you."

His heart raced at that admission—until he realized the "we" part of it.

"We…?" he said.

"Yeah, me and Emma. I'm sure my dad will miss you, too, but he'll never show it."

She laughed, but he shook his head, silencing her.

"Sorry. Maybe I wasn't clear. I'm taking Emma so she can meet him."

Kelsey shot up, her mouth agape.

"You're just taking her? Without talking to me about it?"

Liam frowned and rose to meet her, but she held up a hand as if to say *Stop*.

"I'm talking to you about it *now*, Kels."

"Is that what that suitcase in the cabin is for? You already packed for her?"

He didn't answer, which was all the confirmation she needed.

"First of all you assumed I'd be okay with her going, and second you didn't even think to check with me about what she'll need?"

Now it was his turn to be offended. "I'm her father. I've got a pretty good handle on what our daughter needs for a three-day trip, Kelsey. And I don't need your permission. I'm her dad."

"And I'm her mom. Maybe not legally, like you, but in all the ways that count."

"You have to let her go, Kels. Have a little faith in me."

"I… I don't know how to do that."

"I thought you'd be happy about this. I'm putting aside my grudge so I can be a better man for Emma. For you."

The last two words came out in a whisper, but she'd heard them—he could tell by the shock in her eyes.

"If you cared about me you'd know I'd never be okay with you yanking Emma away without talking to me first. Or, heck—did you think of inviting me?"

"I do care about you—but if you want to play that game, we can, Kels. How can I care about you when you don't trust me as a father? That's my insecurity—you know that, right?"

She stilled, nodding. "And mine is not being

around if something happens to the people I care about."

"Then come with me."

She shook her head and her bottom lip trembled. "I have the Foundation dinner to plan… I can't leave right now."

"So I'm damned if I do and damned if I don't?" he said. "I can't win."

"You can stay."

He saw the pleading in her eyes and he damn near almost gave in.

"My dad is sick, Kelsey. This might be goodbye."

"Oh, God. I'm so sorry. Will he not be okay?"

"I'm not sure. I'll find out tomorrow, though."

"Tomorrow?"

He nodded.

"You're leaving *tomorrow*?"

He nodded again, feeling sillier each time he did. Maybe he should have said something sooner, but he'd never thought she'd have this strong a reaction to a three-day trip.

"And I suppose, since we're just colleagues who screw from time to time, it didn't occur to you to tell me about your dad being sick, either?"

"Now, that's not fair, Kelsey—"

Kelsey stood up, strode to her door and opened it, gesturing to the hallway. "I want you to go, Liam."

He was prepared to make the wrongs he'd committed right, but how could he do that when she wouldn't even meet his gaze?

"Please—"

"No. I mean it."

When she finally looked at him he saw a deep sorrow etched in the corners of her lips and her eyes.

"I can't be with you, Liam. Not if you can't understand where I'm coming from. I need a partner—someone who'll talk to me when things are tough, not just wait for them to smooth out and then fill me in later."

He stared at her, waiting for his vocal cords to jump into action. "That's why I'm going," he said at last. "So I can finally open up to you once this part of my life is behind me."

Tears filled the bottom of her eyes and a few spilled over. His chest almost caved in on itself. He knew he was likely the cause of whatever pain she felt.

"Can't you see, Liam? That's too late."

# CHAPTER THIRTEEN

KELSEY FLIPPED THROUGH the planner on her home office desk, highlighting the items on her to-do list she had yet to conquer before the Foundation dinner. It was just a week away, but that would go quickly.

There were centerpieces to make, but her sister Mari had volunteered for that, since she was the one who'd sucked all the creative genes out of their genetic pool. Kelsey could cross that off.

The guest list was solid, the invitations sent out long ago, and the guest of honor—her first Gold Fleece patient, Mira Yates—had been contacted and her hotel set up. Kelsey should probably check in with everyone who hadn't yet RSVP'd. She'd make the calls herself after lunch.

It was just… Her mind and heart just weren't in it.

Not when it had been a week and a half since she'd seen Liam or Emma.

He'd left a note when she hadn't answered his calls.

*I'm sorry I didn't include you in the decision to visit my father. I have to see him, to introduce him to his granddaughter before it's too late. And I need to make things right with him before I can show up fully for you and Emma.*

*I know that might not make sense to you,*
*but again, I'm going to ask that you trust me.*
*Emma is safe. I'll protect her with my life.*
*Please know that.*
*Liam XO*

That was it.

He was supposed to have been gone three days, but that had turned into a week.

His text had read simply:

Got delayed on this end. Since you aren't answering my calls, I just want you to know it'll be a couple more days while they run tests on my father before his surgery.

Logically, she knew this must be true, but it didn't make it any easier to put aside the worry that plagued her.

What was Emma eating? Drinking?

Was she getting enough Vitamin D? But also enough sunscreen?

Her panic spiraled.

His second text had been just as infuriatingly sweet.

I miss you and Mike and really wish I could talk to you in person.

*In person?* He knew where she lived.

He'd attached a video of Emma, but she didn't have the heart to watch it. Because behind all the other fears a larger one loomed. What if her little girl was thriving without her?

"I don't know how much longer I can do this," she'd lamented to Mike one day, as they'd shopped for groceries.

"He'll be back," her dad had argued. He'd picked up a can of formula, then put it down again with a sigh. "Liam's a good man…"

But even Mike had the telltale signs of exhaustion carved out in the bags under his eyes and the lines around his mouth, which didn't smile as much without Emma. Their sweet girl was the glue holding their small family together, and without her they were both adrift. The only difference was, Kelsey didn't share the same optimism.

"I don't know, Dad. His texts have been few and far between, and he hasn't once mentioned a plan for coming back. What if his dad gets worse? Will he stay away forever?"

"You know, hun, you *could* call him and hash this out."

"I could—but I already said my piece. I'm not putting myself out there again."

Mike had opened his mouth to offer something—probably another one of his "everything will be okay" dad-isms—but Kelsey hadn't wanted to hear it.

"No, not even for Liam."

"What about for Emma?"

Kelsey had sighed and added four avocados to her cart.

*Oh, Emma.*

Liam hadn't just vanished, leaving a space in Kelsey's life the shape of him. He'd taken Emma, too, and the gaping hole left behind by two of the three most important people in her life was consuming her. Nothing filled it—not even throwing herself into making the Foundation dinner the best yet.

She'd booked guest speakers, caterers, and even a balloon animal guy for the kids who would be in attendance. And all this while she'd worked ten, twelve, even fourteen-hour shifts at Mercy.

Delivery after delivery, all she could see was Emma's face in the newborns, all she could hear was Emma's soft cries echoing down the hall. Her love for obstetrics was waning with each moment she spent away from her daughter.

When ten days had passed, Kelsey had gone from worried to despondent. She'd stopped hearing from Liam altogether, and was running out of reasons to get out of bed in the morning. Because Kelsey's greatest fear lived in the quiet from Liam's end: what if she'd given in to chaos and she was losing Emma as a result? She could barely manage losing Liam. To give them both up…

She wouldn't survive it.

Kelsey flipped the page to a secondary list of things she needed to do for the Foundation after the dinner had passed.

"Yeah. Not happening today," she muttered, slamming shut the planner and tossing it in her desk drawer, where it wouldn't taunt her.

She needed some air. She'd been at this for two hours and hadn't made a bit of headway. Maybe if she cleared the Liam-induced fog around her brain she'd have better luck.

*Yeah, right.*

She laid her forehead on the cool veneer of the desk. Letting out a long, slow breath heated her cheeks and released some of the tension in her chest.

"Kels?" her dad called, knocking on her half-open door.

"Yeah?"

She stood up, stretching. It felt good enough that she considered a run, to shed some of the emotional weight that was dragging her down.

As her dad walked into the room a text chimed on her phone. The screen showed her background photo of Emma, sitting in her highchair, her cheeks smeared with avocado. Kelsey placed a hand over her chest. An ache opened up there, threatened to swallow her whole.

The name on the screen didn't help.

*Liam.*

Her fingers itched to see what news he'd sent, if only to put herself out of her misery, but she focused on her dad.

"This little miss wanted to say good morning."

He held up his own phone, and even though Kelsey closed her eyes against the image, her daughter's voice babbled through, worming its way into Kelsey's heart.

"Dad, I can't watch that. It hurts too much."

"Kels, look at me."

She opened her eyes and trained her gaze on her father. But the hazy image of Emma on a play mat not dissimilar to the one in Liam's cabin threatened her focus.

"You're hurtin'. I know it, he knows it, and I'll bet even Emma feels it. But you can't shut them out, hun, no matter what you're feeling."

"What I'm *feeling*? Dad, I've been a fighter all my life. I've never let up. Until I did—handing over Page to a doctor I only knew on reputation. Do you know how horrible I feel, knowing she died on someone else's table? Knowing that she never got to meet her daughter? It's stifling, Dad. But Page is gone, and now my one job is to care for her daughter, so the guilt doesn't eat me alive. But I can't. I can't care for her because she's not here, by my side and safe. And that's killing me."

"I'm sorry you went through all that, Bug. And that you feel so out of control. But you can't control everything."

"Can't I?" she said, as much to herself as her father. "If I work hard enough I can make up for any margin of error. Except with Liam and with Emma."

Her dad paused the video and put down the phone as the tears started falling down her cheeks.

"I asked the right questions… I waited for him to open up with me. And now, like every other time, I'm on the losing end of something wonderful."

"You're not losing, Kels. As far as I can see you still have Emma if you want her. And not just her, either. He's reaching out…trying his best through an awful situation."

Kelsey sniffled and wiped at her nose and cheeks. "How do you know?"

Mike's cheeks turned the same shade of red as his shirt. "I've been keeping in touch with Liam."

Her jaw dropped along with her heart.

"Now, before you say anything, I'm entitled to keep up with Emma. She's my granddaughter, too."

"And she's *my* daughter."

Her father finally met her gaze and she wished he hadn't. What she saw there was a mirror being held up to what she'd just said and how she'd been acting. Whatever ache Liam had opened up in her in the way he'd left, she'd kept digging at it on her own.

"Oh, God. I've messed up, haven't I?"

Her heart had felt close to shattering every time

it beat just moments before, but now it raced as if it was struggling to catch up.

"Will she forgive me?"

Mike nodded, his smile weak and his eyes moist. "Yeah… She's too young to remember you taking your time to work through all this. Every parent has a crisis of faith at some point."

"*Every* parent?"

Mike sniffled and shrugged. "When your mom died, Kels, I… Well, I didn't handle it well."

Kelsey swiped at the tears that just kept on coming. Good grief, how much more could she cry?

"I'm so sorry, Dad."

"Nonsense. I've said it a thousand ways and this time I need you to hear it, hun. It's not your fault."

"But—"

"No 'buts.' Would you blame Emma for Page's death?"

Kelsey gasped in horror at the idea. "Absolutely not." It came out as a whisper, but the words screamed inside her heart. "I'd never blame Emma for what happened."

But didn't she hold herself to a completely different set of standards?

"But if I hadn't come along, you and Mom and Mari—"

"Would have missed out on the best thing in our lives. The kicker is, if your mom was here, she'd agree. There's nothing I'd change about my life except to have you realize you deserve love and happiness the same as everyone else. But you can't will it into happening. You have to let go and have a little faith."

The truth settled in her stomach, but it still hurt.

"Liam said the same thing."

"He's a smart guy."

That was true.

"Anyway, if anyone was to blame back then, it was me. When your mom died, I kinda lost who I was and took off."

"Took off?"

Mike sat down in the chair opposite Kelsey's desk.

"For a month. Your Aunt Peggy kept you and Mari while I got my head right. I felt guilty, leaving you behind, but it was nothing compared to how scared I was to stay."

"Why did you come back?"

Mike's smile was full this time, and Kelsey felt her skin warm seeing it.

"I loved you two something fierce. Always have, always will. When I was good to go I came back, and never left your side again."

Kelsey stood up and hugged her father tight to her chest. "I never knew that."

"Like Emma won't need to know that Liam took two months to feel right before coming to get her... or that you needed this time to figure out what you need."

"Did Liam stop texting because of that? Because I'm too broken and controlling?"

Mike shook his head. "Nope. He doesn't see you that way. But it won't matter until you don't see yourself that way. He's giving you space to figure out his role in your life."

"His role…"

All this time she'd thought he hadn't included her in his plans because she didn't matter. Not that she'd given him a chance to explain himself… But now she wasn't so sure.

"I… I don't know."

"Well, how do you feel about the guy?"

Heat built behind her eyes again. "I love him, Dad. At least I thought I did. But how can that be true if I told him to get out of my office and haven't talked to him since?"

"Love doesn't always act according to its own best interests, Bug. I'm testament to that."

"But what if it is love and he doesn't come back? What if he doesn't choose me?"

God, if she was broken now, she'd be irretrievably so after that.

Mike stood up. "Did he ever give you any reason to think he'll do that? Any *real* reason?" he added, when her face reflected her fear of being kept in the dark.

"No. No, he didn't."

In fact, aside from her father, he was the one person on earth who'd made her feel safe, seen, and cared for. Calm during stormy seas. His failing was only that he'd taken Emma away just when Kelsey had felt they were closing in on something special.

"Okay, then… I'm gonna end my little speech with this."

Kelsey braced herself.

"Trust is easy to give when life's going your way. It's harder to keep when things get tough, but that's when you'll need it most. As long as he's not the one breaking that trust, lean on it to get you through."

Kelsey smiled. "Have you been practicing that speech, Dad? Because you nailed it."

"Nah, just living it revision by revision…trying to get it right in my own life."

"I love you, Dad. And I'll reach out to Liam, I promise. I just have so much to do for this dang dinner. I'm grateful we have the guest numbers we do—it's going to be a record by a long shot—but it means double the work for the board and myself."

*Plus, I need time to process this. I love Liam, but he's not here.*

"Take a break for a minute, Bug. You should see what she's been up to."

Mike pulled out his phone and opened it up to a photo of Liam holding Emma.

Kelsey's breath halted in her lungs and her heart swelled. She hadn't seen his face in days, refusing to look at the photos they'd taken together on her phone, but even if she'd given in it wouldn't have been the same as looking into the eyes of the man staring back at her in this picture.

It was recent. And even though it had only been shy of two weeks since she'd last seen him, Liam was...different. Stronger. It was reflected in his piercing gaze. But also softer, in the way his smile reached his eyes. He looked like Atlas might have if he'd decided to discard the weight of the world.

Whatever he'd been up to, he looked...happy. Content. They both did.

*Without me.*

Kelsey's breathing was uneven, but she worked to steady it. Her anxiety was her burden, and she'd need to let it go if she wanted Liam and Emma in her life for good.

"Go ahead," she said.

Her father clicked on the image, which turned out to be a video.

"Okay, baby girl, say hi to Mommy and Grandpa Mike."

"Grandpa Mike?" Kelsey whispered, raising a brow. But her heart was still trying to process Liam addressing her to Emma as "Mommy."

"Shh... Listen."

"Da!" Emma said, drawing Kelsey's attention back to the video.

"Did she just say—?"

"She did. That's what I came to show you. Well, that and this." He lifted the phone again.

"Who is this?" Liam asked, pointing to himself.

"Da!" Emma said, giggling and pointing to Liam.

Kelsey felt tears on her cheeks, but for the first time in almost a month they came with laughter. Her daughter was thriving, and instead of being something to fear it was *beautiful*.

"And who is this?" Liam asked, pointing to a photo of Kelsey. It was the one he'd framed and put by his bedside.

"Ma!" Emma said, and threw her arms out as if Kelsey might leap out of the photo and catch her— which she desperately wished she could do.

God, she missed diving into her daughter's scent and softness.

"Oh, sweet girl! She's so smart!" Kelsey was half laughing, half crying now, the emotional impact of not just hearing her daughter's first words, but recognizing them for what they were, hitting her with blunt force.

Mom and Dad. Kelsey and Liam. The perfect team. They did work well together—like he'd been telling her all along...

"Isn't she?" Mike said, beaming. "Liam didn't even have to coach her. She did this all on her own. You know what it means, don't you, hun?"

Kelsey cocked her head.

"It means you're a mom, Kels. Like you always wanted and always deserved."

Kelsey choked on a sob. "Dad—" she started, her voice catching.

"No," he interrupted. "I don't care. You and Emma are amazing and both of you have been through so much. You deserve to be happy."

"What if it's too late?" Kelsey asked.

"It isn't. Love is never too late. It comes to us right on time, every time. Look at Kris. And now you and Liam."

Her dad saw right through to her real question— *What if I've pushed him away and he doesn't want me anymore?*

"Give him a call, Bug. I can't promise things will be better than normal, but who knows?"

Kelsey let that sink in as her dad left the room, a chirping Emma shouting "Ma! Da!" down the hallway as he replayed the video.

"Normal" was falling asleep on Liam's chest, with Emma in the room next door. It was waking up to kisses from a man who truly saw her for who she was, flaws and all, and who still wanted to plant his lips all over her body.

*I wouldn't mind "normal."*

Her dad's final advice to Kelsey that day was the only thing to upset her good mood.

"Lemme know if you need help, but I know you'll be throwing a helluva Gold Fleece event. Those women need you, hun."

If she was going to do that, she couldn't think about Liam—or how much she cared about him.

It would distract her from the work that had to be done for the charity patients she cared most about. The ones who'd started her down this path.

*I have to do this so I know I'm worthy of him. And Emma.*

Kelsey was buoyed with a sense of optimism she hadn't had in weeks. Months… Heck, close to a year. Her dad had been right about one thing: she deserved a family and so did all the women Kelsey could help with Gold Fleece. And to make that happen she'd have to start letting go. Of fear, of her firm grip, and of her mistakes.

Her heart spoke to her now, and it cried out that, while Emma's new vocabulary was indeed cause to celebrate, it would be, oh, so much sweeter to celebrate as a family.

*Liam*, it whispered to her. *You love Liam and nothing will ever be worth anything if you can't fix it with him and give you two an honest shot.*

It might not go the way she wanted it to, but— Foundation dinner looming or not—she knew she had to try. Because she finally understood that she and Emma deserved a happily-ever-after. And that included Liam—for both of them.

# CHAPTER FOURTEEN

LIAM GAZED OUT over the city of Austin, the high-rises and office buildings rolling like metallic waves toward the horizon. It didn't offer him anything near the same peace of mind as the view of the Pacific Ocean from Kelsey's balcony.

Nothing could give him that, though. Nothing except…well, Kelsey's balcony. And Kelsey.

His chest had been plagued with a physical ache since he'd flown out of LAX ten days ago. It wasn't heartburn or stress, like he might suggest to a patient who presented with the same symptoms. No, it was *heartbreak*, plain and simple.

He never should have left Kelsey—not when she was so scared of what it might mean. And he should have included her—she was right about that. But he had to make things right with his dad if he ever wanted a chance with her.

And they'd made progress—slow and steady, like his father's chemo treatments.

What wasn't groundbreaking so much as self-realization was the fact that Liam's father wasn't the actual problem Liam had thought he was. It was Liam who had continuously allowed his father to guide his decisions—even by rebelling, and choosing something his father would never approve of, Liam had been led by him.

Once he'd realized that, little truth bombs had

kept hitting him upside the head. What if he'd set out to get everything he'd ever wanted and got it? What if he'd figured out he didn't need his old man's approval?

*Huh... Go figure.*

God, Liam had made a mess of things, hadn't he? Even though he'd spent a month treating his PTSD, it turned out he had a lot of other work still to do.

He ran a hand through his hair and exhaled on a three count.

"Son?" a voice called from the doorway.

"Hey, Dad. I'm in here."

It was new, the way Liam smiled when his dad came in the room, but it was a welcome change for sure.

"You ready for the board meeting?"

"I am. Thanks for calling them together for this. It means a lot to me."

*And to the woman I care about more than almost anything.*

His dad shook his head, as if to say it was nothing—another strange but welcome side effect of the past week. The other side effects were less visible but just as promising: the cancer was shrinking. For better or worse, Liam would get some time with his old man.

"Just make sure you highlight to them the ways they can save money and still get Everson Health the recognition they want," his father said. "Some of us may be emotionally invested, but they'll still want the numbers."

"I have them here."

He handed them to his dad, whose sharp gaze hadn't wavered even during his treatments.

He pored over them. "This looks great, Liam. Good work. I know I've said it a lot since you got here, but thank you for coming and…well, giving me the chance to do this. To meet her."

He nodded in the direction of Emma's guest suite, where she was napping.

"Of course. I wish I would have known about the procedure earlier, though. Or that you were sick."

Even now, having known about his father's stage three pancreatic cancer for two and a half weeks, it still made him nauseated. He'd wasted so much time being mad at the man—time he wouldn't get back.

*But you couldn't have made him come to the table to talk on your timeline. He came to you when he was ready.*

That was true. And at least they had time now.

"I didn't want our meeting to be all about that. Cancer or not, I wanted to meet Emma and make things right with you. I'm sorry it took me so damn long."

"It happened when it needed to. And now you'll get to know both my girls."

He couldn't wait to introduce his father to Kelsey. The day couldn't come soon enough for so many reasons. Most of all because he missed the woman's arms around him—enough that he'd taken to sleeping with one of Emma's towels, which smelled like Kelsey.

*Yeah, I know it's pathetic*, he told his subconscious, before it could say something snarky.

Liam's dad met his gaze. "You're happy."

It was a statement, not a question.

"I am."

"Good. That's all I wanted. I know it doesn't mean much, coming from me, but despite my influence you're a fine dad, Liam. A fine dad."

"Thank you, Dad. It does mean something."

Enough that his eyes watered, anyway.

"Dr. Everson?" Nadine, his father's receptionist, called from the doorway, knocking to announce her entrance into the suite.

"She's talking to you," Liam's dad said, smiling.

"Come on in," Liam told her, stealing a glance at his watch.

He had twenty minutes until he was supposed to meet with his dad's board about the project he'd put into play with Kris from Mercy before he'd left. She'd be the key to approving a larger site on Mercy's campus and help finding doctors to staff it afterwards. Any distraction from the focus of his thoughts these past two weeks—his dad's health, Kelsey's feelings, and his own plans for the future—was a welcome one.

"You've got a phone call, sir."

Liam nodded and took the phone from Nadine.

"I'll see you in a few?" he told his father, who nodded and left.

It was still awkward between them from time to time—like that morning, when his father hadn't been sure where to sit at the dining table because Liam had chosen the formal space to drink his coffee and feed Emma. His dad had wandered between different spots, putting his plate down and picking it up before moving it again. Finally, Liam had tapped the chair next to him and gestured that his dad should sit there, with him and Emma.

But they'd made more progress than regression.

Funny how things worked out… His plan to come home had inadvertently carved out a direct path to Kelsey, and it would now help her expand her Foundation in the ways she'd told him she'd dreamt of. The trick would be working with her fears about relinquishing control. Especially after losing Page. The last thing he wanted was to try and honor his late wife's memory by giving Kelsey what he imagined she wanted most, only to alienate her by pushing too far, too fast in the process.

Speaking of Kelsey…he'd made some strides there, too. Specifically, giving a name to what he felt for her. It was love—plain and simple. He loved the stubborn, determined, beautiful woman. And, as much as for her being good for Emma, he wanted Kelsey for himself, too. If she'd have him.

Liam smiled as he answered the phone. He still had a long way to go, but he'd come pretty far.

"Hello?" he said into the phone.

"Hey, Liam. It's Mike."

The smile on Liam's face deepened. "Mike. I was just thinking about you." *And your daughter.*

"Just checking in and giving you an update. How's Austin?"

"Hot as hell, but with better food."

Mike chuckled. "I don't mean to tempt you, but it's a balmy seventy-four degrees here, and the sun reflecting off the water is just begging for a rod and some bait."

"Three days, Mike. Three days."

"Good to hear, son. I'm proud of you for taking care of your family. It was a tough call to leave, but I know our girls will thank you for it when they have two grandpas to spoil them. Thanks for that video, by the way."

Liam let slide the comment about "our girls" because otherwise it would override everything he was trying to do—namely, make sure he did things right this time. If he skipped any of the steps in front of him he'd trip up sometime in the future, and that wouldn't be fair to the women he loved.

"Of course, Mike. So, what can I do you for?"

"Well, I was hoping Kelsey would be the one to call you, but she said she had some errands to run and I thought you should know."

"What's that?" Liam checked his watch again. Only fifteen minutes.

"Well, two things. First one's less awe-inspiring. Kels has changed the seating chart for the Foundation dinner and opened up a space next to her."

"For you?"

"Nope. I'm on her other side. And her sister can't make it. So that only leaves one thought in my mind… You planning on coming?"

"I wouldn't miss it."

And if it turned out that seat wasn't for him— well, he had other reasons for showing up that night that superseded sitting next to a beautiful doctor while she raised money to help moms in need. If he took care of the last few items on his to-do list there was an offer he had to make her. Two offers, really.

For the first time, his future prospects excited him.

"Good to hear it. We miss you, son. You have a second to talk about something else?" Mike asked.

"Sure. I've got time."

*The only thing on his docket the rest of the day was the meeting to finalize Kelsey's dream project, but he had a few minutes to kill beforehand.*

"She misses you, you know. She walks up to the cabin every night, turns on the porch light, and the next morning walks back and turns it off. She doesn't think I see her, but a father knows things. You'll see that yourself someday."

What could Liam possibly say to Mike that

wouldn't result in him crying like Emma when she knocked over her blocks? Kelsey was literally leaving a light on for him.

*It wasn't much to go off, but it was enough.*

Was it too much to hope she loved him back?

"That's great, Mike. I promise I'll use the information for good, not evil." Mike laughed. "And thanks for letting me know you got the video. She's changing every day, isn't she?"

"That she is. You got a special one there, son."

*Was Mike still talking about Emma, or another special female in his life?*

"I do. At least I hope I do."

He didn't have to clarify that it wasn't Emma he meant. Mike knew. He'd become a father figure to Liam in a matter of two months—further proof that being related by blood and good parenting didn't necessarily go hand in hand. Kelsey had made him believe it at first, Mike soon after.

"I promise I hear you, and that I'm doing everything in my power to fix what I started."

"That's why I love you, son."

Mike's voice cracked along with Liam's resolve.

"At the risk of you taking that back, you should know I love Kelsey. Heck, thinking of her and taking care of Emma is the only thing that gets me through my days. If I can make her see that, I will…but if I have to choose between her happiness and my own—well, you should know she'll win every time."

"I'll leave you to that, then. Godspeed, Liam."

"Right back at you, Mike. And thanks for your help. See you Friday."

"Yup. And don't forget a suit. This thing calls for fancy duds."

"Got it."

Liam hung up, the image of Kelsey in an evening gown seizing his imagination before he could shake it loose.

*No time for that.*

He wanted to help Kelsey see the good she could do by putting her fears aside and chasing her dreams, while at the same time supporting her through that realization as she had done for him. And to add to that he couldn't wait to show her just how ready he was for a relationship that would honor what they had.

And that meant he had way too much to do.

Starting with this board meeting and ending with shopping for a suit that would draw the attention of a certain doctor who'd changed his life and for whom he was hoping to return the favor.

# CHAPTER FIFTEEN

KELSEY CHECKED AND rechecked her small clutch four times before deciding to ditch the lipstick and bring a smaller lip balm instead. How did women do this whole small purse thing? Give her a backpack any day over this chic nonsense...

She spun in front of the mirror, assessing the whole ensemble.

Her dress, though wholly out of her comfort zone, was perfect. She'd fought with Mari about the frivolous purchase when they'd been at the checkout counter of Saks, but now...

The silver sequins draped over curves she usually kept hidden beneath scrubs. And the deep V of the front of the dress mirrored the backless aspect that had sold Kelsey on it in the store.

*Yeah, it was worth every penny.*

She was also glad she'd allowed Mari to pull her hair into a loose knot, giving her a sort of sexy I've-tried-but-don't-want-you-to-think-I-have look.

*If only a certain trauma surgeon would be there tonight to make the whole thing worth the effort.*

She'd left him a seat beside her, but her hopes weren't that high. She'd never called him, and he'd only reached out through Mike.

But God, if he came...it would mean so much to her. Especially if he brought Emma, the tie that bound them as much as their feelings for each other.

She missed her baby girl so much, but they could survive without each other—and knowing that gave Kelsey strength.

Nerves fluttered in her stomach, taking flight up her chest and neck as she considered how far she'd come but what she still had to do. She had to tell Liam the truth—she wanted a life *with* him. No more hiding behind the veil of "co-parenting."

Kelsey now believed she was worthy of love, of a family, of being a mother. But asking for it was something else altogether. If she didn't, though, she'd never be happy—that much was true.

Her app alerted her that her car was there. Her dad had said he would meet her at the venue, claiming he had some errands to run—their catch-all family phrase for *Don't ask me about it*. His words from the day Liam had sent that video came back to her as she slipped out of the front door.

*"It's possible for you to feel two things at the same time. You can be happy about the fresh start you got with Emma and still want more for yourself. That just makes you human. I want you to have not what I had, but your version of that. Whatever fulfillment looks like to you."*

An image came to her of Liam leaning on an elbow in her bed, gazing down at her with what she now recognized as love. Emma peacefully sleeping between them.

And one of herself, helping patients realize that same fulfillment.

All of this came to her mind and she smiled.

She was ready for that life, and could only hope Liam would accept her apology for putting her issues on him.

The driver pulled up to the front of the convention center and the moment Kelsey stepped out of the car reporters clamored to talk to her about her work with the Gold Fleece and the women she'd helped. She saw her dad standing off to the side, beaming at each reporter's kind comments.

*She did good work.*

It was high time she admitted it. And part of that came with releasing the guilt she carried deep in her chest over Page's death.

"I miss, you, Page," she whispered. "You'd love this, too. All the glitz you used to laugh at on Hollywood Boulevard under one roof. We even got *you-know-who* to come."

"Who you talking to, hun?" asked her father.

"Page," she admitted. "You made it," she said, hugging her dad.

"Of course. I wouldn't miss this, Bug. I'm proud enough to pop. She'd have loved this, wouldn't she? Page, I mean."

"I was thinking the same thing. And it helps, knowing as much. I miss her, but I can't let that keep me from moving on. I guess that's part of why I was talking to her—I'd love her permission to keep her in my heart but move on."

"You know she gave that to you the day she passed, hun. The rest is up to you. So get to it, huh?"

Kelsey laughed. "Thanks, Dad. For being there for Emma, so I could keep all this up for the Foundation. They're both so important to me, but I couldn't have been successful at either without your help."

He beamed, his cheeks looking especially rosy.

When they were finally in the foyer, Kelsey gasped. The events company had nailed it. Gold tapestries fell from the ceilings and were embroidered with the name of every woman and child who had been a recipient of the charity's help and—well, there were dozens. Close to a hundred.

The expansive room was filled from wall to wall with those families, and also the wealthy donors who made Kelsey's program possible, and when they saw her, they broke into applause. Kelsey scanned the crowd, her eyes searching for one face in particular, but if he was there he was hidden amongst the masses.

Kris came up to her, Owen on her arm, both of them clapping. "You've done an amazing thing here, Kelsey."

"Thanks, Kris. The events company does great work."

"I meant your Foundation. I see its results in the hospital, but with it all laid out here at one time… We're lucky to have you, Dr. Gaines. Very lucky indeed."

"Thank you, Kris."

"The pleasure's mine. Let's get something on the books next week and discuss how Mercy can help to bring this Foundation to a national level. How's that sound?"

Kelsey could only smile and nod, like a kid who'd gotten the pony she desired at Christmas. She was nervous about relinquishing control of her charity to others, but if they were the right people it could work. And she had a lot of the right people in her corner. Including Mercy, whose reputation would give the Foundation instant national recognition, if not financial viability. Liam's support had already shown her the possibilities that outweighed the fears. She had no doubt he'd be in her corner if she pursued this dream—as a colleague at least. And knowing that fortified her even more than her private memories of Page.

"Um...great. Again, thanks."

*You've said that, silly. Three times. Move on.*

Her pride broke through the last remaining barrier that was trying to tell Kelsey she didn't deserve to be *this* happy, that she didn't deserve love *and* a family *and* a career that fulfilled her.

*She did—at least as much as anyone else.*

If only she could take back the words she'd used to push away her handsome ex-Army medic a couple weeks ago.

She shivered.

The air in L.A. was never cool at this time of year, but the hotel's air conditioning made it feel like winter by the water. She rubbed at her arms and tried to find her footing as the crowds dissipated, leaving her to stand in a receiving line of sorts. Kelsey felt rudderless in the sea of people all jockeying for time with her.

"We just want to thank you for all you do for the young mothers of America," a woman in her fifties told Kelsey.

Her lanyard indicated that she was part of an abuse shelter Kelsey partnered with.

"You're such an inspiration," said a socialite whom Kelsey had helped get pregnant, and then delivered the baby. "Please let me know how I can stay involved in this program and what you need to keep it open. You do so much good, Dr. Gaines."

"I just want you to know Bill and I are grateful to be a part of this, Dr. Gaines," said another woman. "We wouldn't have Tyler if it wasn't for you."

Claustrophobia inched closer to Kelsey, but she kept a smile on her face through each platitude and good wish from a guest. This was why she was there—why the whole Gold Fleece program existed.

When another hand sat on her shoulder she readied her smile, prepared to greet another Gold Fleece family or donor. Instead, she turned and found herself gazing into gold and chestnut eyes and looking at a smile that arrested her heart on the spot. There, touching her and making her wish the rest of the guests would evaporate on the spot, so she could be alone with this man, was the very handsome, very kind and very distracting Army medic she'd been daydreaming about for weeks.

"Liam…" she whispered.

His eyes danced with the pleasure of catching her off guard. He nodded.

"I just want to thank you for keeping my amazing daughter safe until I could meet her. You made my family complete."

The words were simple enough, and to a bystander no different than anything else people were lining up to tell her. But the way his hand slid down her arm, the intonation of his voice, even the gentle smile that welcomed her back as if she hadn't shoved him away from her—all of it meant so much more than what he'd said.

Only then did she glance down and see the soft gold tufts of hair and the plump arms of the only other person Kelsey cared to see. *Emma.* When she noticed Emma's outfit—a sparkling gold dress with a matching bow—she laughed despite the moisture behind her eyes.

"Oh, sweet girl. You have no idea how much I missed you."

She kissed the top of her daughter's head and inhaled her scent. When she reached for Emma he met her halfway, depositing the infant in her arms as his arm draped around her hip. Just like that, all the pain and uncertainty of the past two weeks evaporated. No matter what came next, Kelsey had everything she wanted at that moment.

"Thank you for taking such good care of her, Liam."

# CHAPTER SIXTEEN

KELSEY'S SKIN WAS flushed the color red he'd come to associate with her blush, which aroused him to no end. Did she have any idea how stunning she was in that dress? Holding their daughter? And she'd told him he'd done well. Damn, he might not make it till the end of the night to share his plans with her.

He swallowed hard, so he wouldn't be tempted to hand Emma off to Mike and crush his lips into Kelsey's, to take her in his arms right there and strip her out of the slinky silver fabric that hung on curves that called to him like a siren's song. All that flesh…just begging to be touched. All that skin… just asking for his tongue to taste it…

But not yet. Not until he'd said what he needed to say and made sure Kelsey knew what was in his heart, not just on his mind.

"Did you miss me?" he asked.

Her eyes widened and her mouth opened just enough that he could see her perfect white teeth. Teeth that had raked over his chest more than once. He'd known how difficult it would be to see this woman in person again, to touch her and smell the floral aroma she carried with her, but he'd underestimated just how hard by several degrees.

"I… I did. Very much, in fact. I'm just surprised… I figured with the way I treated you, you might not come home…"

*Home. And she'd mentioned it first.*

Hope trickled to the surface of his thoughts.

"I needed to make things right," he told her.

"I know that now. I'm sorry about your father."

"And I'm sorry I didn't include you in my decision to go back to Austin. Or to take Emma."

"Why didn't you?"

"I didn't know what I was walking into or what I'd feel. And I'm sorry. That's not a good enough reason, but I will always include you in the future. Because no matter what I do the rest of my life, none of it will be right without *you*, Kels."

She opened her mouth to reply but he shook his head.

"Please don't disagree with me. I know I haven't been honest with you before now, but I love you, Kelsey. And I'm ready to talk about our future if it's not too late."

Her eyes became emerald saucers, and *darn* if the way they sparkled under the chandeliers wasn't alluring as heck… But he needed to get this out before he lost his nerve.

"Will you hear me out?"

"Yes. No. I mean, yes, I'd like to talk, and, no, it's not too late."

She looked like she wanted to add something, but then the lights dimmed, like they did in a theater performance.

"Um…that's my cue. Can we meet after dinner? There are some things I need to say as well."

"Of course."

His brain went into overdrive, trying to figure out what she wanted to talk about. Her smile was genuine, but her request had been vague enough to make him question—well, everything.

*Some things I need to say as well.*

"Let's meet back here when you're done."

"That sounds perfect. I'm looking forward to it."

And there was that glimmer of hope, always waiting in the wings.

"Oh, can I take her up with me?" she asked. "I'd like people to see her."

"Of course."

Kelsey walked away, Emma still in her arms, and Liam recalled what his old platoon sergeant had used to say about his own wife: *"I hate for her to leave, but I love to watch her go."*

The dress Kelsey wore obliterated any good sense he'd had left. He was willing to lose it all to be with her. Hopefully, if all went according to plan tonight, he wouldn't have to.

"Liam?" she said suddenly, turning back around to face him.

Her gold hair reflected the crystalline light, shimmering as if of its own accord. She was ethereal. There wasn't another word for it.

"Yeah?"

"I'm really glad you came tonight. It wouldn't be the same without you here."

He smiled, and the yearning in his chest took flight, prancing around and whispering *Told you so* to his overactive sense of pessimism. Love and family hadn't always worked in his favor, but maybe—just maybe—things were turning around.

Liam couldn't keep the grin off his face.

At the front of the room was a floor-to-ceiling screen behind a podium. It flipped through photos of newborns, pregnant women, and families with young kids. It was a visual representation of Kelsey's work. Pride bloomed in his chest.

"I want to thank you all for being here tonight," Kelsey began, addressing the hundreds of guests in the ballroom from the podium.

Her shoulders were back, her posture strong and steady.

*She belonged up there.*

Even Emma looked regal, and seemed to sense this wasn't the time to try and get Kelsey to play with her.

"This is a special night for so many reasons. First, because this is the third anniversary of the Gold Fleece charity named and designed to wrap our patients in love. Second, because we've tripled our donations, meaning we can more than quadruple our accommodations, our treatment centers and our patients. All thanks to you!"

The crowd erupted in cheers and applause, and

Liam joined in from his vantage point next to Mike. On stage, Emma clapped her hands and giggled when the crowd boomed with applause. She, like her mom, was made for this. The world of obstetrics—and his own world—would be so much worse off without Kelsey in it.

Only one pain sliced through an otherwise perfect evening. Liam's heart constricted as he considered the one face not there. *Page's*. It would probably always be that way—the pain of grief reaching out to remind him of all he'd lost. But that pain was numbed by his love and desire for a future with his daughter and a woman he couldn't imagine living without. A woman who'd turned Liam into a man and a father.

As if to punctuate this thought, Kelsey bent down and kissed Emma's head before she introduced the infant. The crowd roared with delight.

When her speech was over, Kelsey joined them. Emma smiled up at Liam with the same wide grin as Kelsey.

"Da!" Emma said, throwing herself against his chest.

His heart swelled and he smiled. "So, talk to me, Dr. Gaines. What's been on your mind?"

She gazed up at him, her green eyes sparkling even more than the dress she wore—which was to say a lot.

"It's hard to recall with you standing there looking dapper in that suit and holding my favorite human," she teased, trailing her finger down the smooth fabric of his sleeve.

Tingles raced along the path she made.

"Then allow me. Kelsey, I want you to know I heard you." He turned to face her, handing Emma to Mike, who slid off towards the dance floor, humming and twirling Emma while she squealed with glee. "Not just about opening up to you, but about what you want out of life as well."

"Did your trip...do what you hoped?"

Liam shrugged. "It's hard to put into words what happened. I should have talked to my father when I first got home, but I was so angry with him. I let that dictate so many of my decisions. It's why... It's why I was afraid to pursue anything with you sooner. Because of his limitations as a husband and a father."

"And now?"

"Now I feel like there's nothing I can't do if I have you and Emma by my side." His lips desperately wanted to kiss her, but not yet. He was close, but there were still some things he needed to do first.

"You do have us, Liam. We're here."

She leaned into him, testing his resolve to keep his hands off her until he was done. He inhaled her scent and it acted like a whiskey shot, going straight into his bloodstream. He'd rather get drunk off her than a highball any day...

"My dad says he owes you an apology he'd like

to make in person. It will be some time until he can travel, so he wanted me to light the way. If you'll hear him out, he'd love to talk to you."

"Of course." Emma nodded. "Especially if it will help him get to know Emma. That's all I wanted for Page—to fix things with him for Emma's sake. God, I feel like I've missed so much."

Liam rubbed her arms, wishing he could take her into his and never let go. "I know—and I'm sorry. I just didn't see a way around that. I'll make it up to you."

"You don't need to do that. If you're okay…well, then I am, too. Anyway, did you fix things? You and your father?"

"We did, thanks. We may never be like you and Mike, but we've come to an understanding."

"Are you…are you going back to Austin after tonight?"

"Nope. I'm here to stay, Kels. Which leads me to the first thing I have to tell you. Ask you, actually. Aside from working out our relationship, I needed my father's help with a project. He came through— which means it's up to you now."

Liam sighed, watching the guests dance and drink—guests whose lives Kelsey had made infinitely richer and filled with love. His life wasn't so different from theirs in that way…

"There's more than just you being back?" she asked.

"Much more."

He couldn't hold back any longer. He tipped her chin up and met her lips with his. It was a soft kiss filled with all his love for this woman. It was a promise of what was to come if she accepted him back into her life.

"Kelsey, my dad is willing—with my help and your permission—to put the full weight of Everson Health behind the Gold Fleece Foundation and support three new locations for its facilities."

Where before there'd been her strong presence, now there was just…space. She'd stepped back, her hand pressed to her chest and her mouth open in surprise. Any ache he'd felt to kiss her was magnified by a thousand.

"Liam…it's…it's too much. I'm not sure I'm ready…"

"To take this on without getting overwhelmed? I'll help hire all the best physicians—physicians you will interview and approve. None of this will happen without you—"

"No. It's just so much…so fast. Kris has already asked if I'll discuss Mercy helping with it, but that's different than having it all set up already."

"Then we'll discuss it. And we'll take as long as you need to feel comfortable. This is your project, your dream. I only want to give you the gift of support to make it happen, but if you're not ready we can wait. I just thought… I thought it might be a way we could honor Page. Maybe name one of the centers after her."

Kelsey glanced around the room at the hundreds of families who had been helped by her dream. As if she'd been waiting to hear it, her subconscious chimed in, sounding an awful lot like Page.

*You've got all the support you need to make your dream come true. Don't let fear keep you from great things, Kelsey. Chase this life down and take everything it has to offer.*

Kelsey smiled. The voice was right. She could do this—especially with the love and support of the man standing beside her. He'd never let her make a decision that would hurt anyone, and she had to trust that. She had to trust that if she let go of control it would be okay. Because it would.

"That's an amazing idea. But can I run the offer by Kris? She's already offered help from Mercy. But thank you, Liam, for making it possible."

"I thought you might want to talk to her, and you should know she's already agreed. But only if it's what you want." He brought out a thin envelope from his jacket pocket and handed it to her. "This is our proposal."

"Is that what you were discussing in her office?"

Liam smiled and nodded. "That and me taking a little time out to see my dad while he got his first round of chemo. Please don't feel rushed into deciding about the Foundation. I just want you to know the support is there, whenever you're ready for it. *If* you're ready for it. I'm not going anywhere, Kels, no matter what you decide."

"Thank you so much, Liam. I'm more grateful than you'll ever know."

Kelsey took the envelope and squeezed Liam tightly. He loved this woman so much, and wanted her happiness above anything else. And he planned to prove that—no matter what she decided about his offer to expand the Foundation.

Because the last trick up Liam's sleeve was a question that would make Kelsey and Emma his family, and he couldn't wait to ask it.

# CHAPTER SEVENTEEN

KELSEY LEAFED THROUGH the papers Liam had given her while her father, Liam, Owen, and Kris looked on. In the background, the DJ was announcing the last song of the night, but there were only a few hangers-on who would need to be corralled into cabs. Everyone else had eaten, danced, and drunk their fill, then headed home or to fancier parties only the truly rich and famous could afford to attend.

A few of the Gold Fleece families were staying the weekend at the hotel as Kelsey's guests. She'd made sure they had tickets to the L.A. Zoo, the Hollywood Stars tour, and of course a fancy dinner. It was one of the best perks of her Foundation—a weekend getaway before delivery, as well as trips away for the annual Foundation dinner.

It was hard to imagine anything better than the proposal in front of her. On paper, it was genius. Mothers in the South and Midwest wouldn't have to travel as far to get access to good medical care, and with the support of Everson Health she—*they*—could help so many more families. More than all that combined, she and Liam would be honoring Page's memory.

"It's going to make your mark on charitable

healthcare," said Liam. "In a good way. Hell, Kelsey, this is everything you wanted."

"I know. It's amazing."

It was. And the most amazing part was knowing she was genuinely ready to take this on. Somehow, over the past two months, she'd grown and changed under the support of her family—Liam included.

"And you're sure you're willing to take this on with her, Liam?" Kris asked. "It's not a small undertaking, running a national foundation."

"I'm ready for it, Kris. I've got contacts in all three locations and my dad's got Everson hospitals there, too, so investment will be minimal. Besides, Kelsey and I make a good team," he said.

He winked at her, and the familiar flip of her stomach came the way it always did when Liam was close to her. Or winked at her. Or she just thought about him.

*Yeah, she was a goner.*

Kelsey placed a hand on his forearm, and even with the thick suit fabric acting as a barrier between his skin and hers she felt the familiar jolt of attraction surge between them.

"Okay. I'll get our team on board. You'd better be prepared to be in my office on Monday, Liam."

Liam laughed, and the flip of Kelsey's stomach quickened.

"I'll see you there, ma'am."

Kris nodded at Owen, who guided them both to the bar.

Mike announced that he was taking Emma home.

And just like that Kelsey was left alone with Liam.

The room seemed to close in on them while the possibilities multiplied.

"How are you?" she asked.

"Better than ever. And looking forward to this," he said, lifting up the papers. "I'm just sorry I left you behind when you needed me."

"I wanted to talk to you about that, actually—" she started, but then the DJ's voice came over the speaker and announced that he was playing one more song—a request from one of the guests.

When "Danny's Song" came on, Kelsey gasped.

"A favorite?" he asked.

"My mom's. It was her and my dad's wedding song."

Liam held out his hand and she took it without asking what he was doing or where he was leading her. By now her heart was leading the way and it would follow him anywhere.

"Dr. Gaines, may I have the honor of this dance?" he asked, when they got to the edge of the dance floor.

"Of course, Dr. Everson."

Liam pulled her close and she inhaled deeply when he hugged her against his chest. The all too familiar scent he wore—like sea air and woodsmoke and cinnamon rolled into one—reached down and tugged at the part of her that was petrified to follow through on what her father had all but demanded of her. That she live her life and make herself happy.

*Liam made her happy.*

Deliriously so. But that scared her, too. Because so much would change, regardless of whether he loved her back. But that was life—full of times when her faith would be tested. Now at least she knew she was strong enough to pass the tests as they arose.

"Liam?"

She stepped up on her toes to close the distance between them. Even with her heels it wasn't enough, so she pulled his head down to hers and kissed him. She didn't care if it was their last kiss or the first of many, just that she got to taste the love and promise on his lips at least once more.

When she pulled back, her eyes were wide. Coffee…and hops. It was like tasting her favorite meal and feeling like she could never have enough of it.

"I don't want you in the cabin anymore."

His eyes went wide and he nodded. "I respect that, Kelsey. I wish it wasn't how you felt, but—"

"I want you to move in with me, Liam. I want to make room for you in my bed and make space in the closet for your things. I want you, period."

"Wait… Are you saying yes, then?"

Now it was her turn to be confused. "To the proposal? Yes, of course. You're right about all the good it can do, and I'm ready—"

"No, not to the proposal," he said, pulling away from her embrace.

Her arms missed his waist, and her waist missed his arms. But none of that mattered as Liam knelt in front of her, his eyes as bright as flecks of gold held under a light.

"What…what are you doing?" Her hands trembled and he kissed them.

"I'm asking a question I'm hoping you've already given the answer to. Kelsey Gaines, I love you. And taking that space in your bed and your closet and your life will be the easiest thing I've ever done in my life. I know we started our relationship on rocky ground, but I also see clearer than ever that my future depends on your happiness. You make me smile, you challenge me, you heal everything that hurts—literally, if you remember the hamstring." He laughed.

*How could she forget? Her hands on his leg for the first time, his shirtless torso taking up all the space in her living room… Yeah, she remembered.*

"Liam…" she began. Her breath was ragged and her stomach was flipping like a clown in the circus.

"I've got so much more to say," he interrupted. "But I'll make it quick. Because I can't wait to kiss you again. Kelsey, Page made me a father, but you taught me about passion and fighting for what you love. You made me a dad. And as it turns out, what I love most is *you*. If you and Emma would do me the honor of being my family, I'll never leave you again."

At these last words Liam pulled a small box from his breast pocket and opened it. Kelsey couldn't see what was inside because her eyes were flooding with tears. All she could do was nod.

When he took something out of the box and slid it on her finger, the people remaining in the room erupted in cheers.

Kelsey looked down at her hand and at the diamond sitting atop a white gold band nestled on her finger. She pulled Liam up and back into her arms. She kissed him again and felt the power of his arms as they wrapped around her.

*He was hers.*

Somehow, even when she'd been afraid of what it would mean to want this as badly as she wanted it now, she'd ended up with her very own happily-ever-after, with a man who was promising to stay forever.

"So, *are* you saying yes, then?" he asked again.

She laughed through the happy tears still sliding down her cheeks. He rubbed them dry with the pad of his thumb and cupped her face for another kiss.

"Yes," she whispered against his lips. "We'll marry you."

As Liam picked her up and twirled her she thought of her father, and all he'd lost so she could have this moment. Somewhere her mother was smiling down at them and giving her approval. And even Page had helped Kelsey find a way through the loss. Her whole family was there, supporting and loving her.

With that thought, Kelsey kissed her husband-to-be and whispered, "Take me home, Dr. Everson."

She was in the mood to start off that happily-ever-after as soon as possible.

# CHAPTER EIGHTEEN

"TELL ME THAT'S not the cake for Emma."

Liam laughed. Kelsey's arms were full of a six-layered sheet cake with an enormous dinosaur on top. Maybe a brontosaurus.

"Oh, it is. But she gets a smaller version for her smash cake. This is more for our guests than for her."

Was it just him, or was his wife growing more beautiful every day? Even in the midst of expanding the Foundation to its three new locations, she still looked calm. Put-together. Happy.

The idea that he had anything to do with the soft smile on her face brought him more joy than he deserved. But he was trying not to think about it that way. He got to experience her love, and he'd spend the rest of his life making her as happy as he could. That was his pleasure and his penance, and he took both seriously.

*Well, not too seriously.*

"Please explain the concept of a smash cake, my love."

She giggled. "Later. Right now, I have to get this cake table set up, and then I want to show you the gift I got for Emma."

"I thought we agreed on the stuffed brachiosaurus?"

It still amazed him that their now one-year-old

loved the gigantic beasts as much as she did. Their little paleontologist in the making.

"We did, but I…um… I have something else as well. I just want to show you before the rest of the guests arrive. When Mari's kids get here the pandemonium won't let up until they leave. Oh, and remind me to pick up those bowls of candy from the table. Otherwise they'll be gone in seconds."

"Have I told you how much I love you?" Liam asked.

He waited for Kelsey to put down the cake and pulled her in for a deep kiss.

*Good grief, did his want for this woman know no bounds?*

He glanced outside the cabin, where they'd moved until they could buy something smaller than the main house and sell this property. His dad and Mike were at the grill, Emma in his father's arms. Kris and Owen were bringing out the side dishes. It was perfect. Everything he'd never known he always wanted.

"Hey, while they're busy, wanna take a little break and… I dunno…make Emma a baby sister? Or at least enjoy practicing?"

He squeezed Kelsey's butt and she whacked his hand with a dishtowel.

"Come with me," she said, crooking her finger at him to follow.

"Yes, ma'am."

She led him down the hallway, but before they got to the master suite she stopped at Emma's room.

"I mean, I guess it's the one room here we haven't christened. And if you really wanna…"

She playfully tossed the dishtowel at him again. "I do *not*, Dr. Everson."

"Then why are we here, Dr. Gaines-Everson?" he teased, wrapping his arms around her from behind. "Because I intend to make love to you in the next thirty seconds. So if you want our bed, let me carry you there."

Were her breasts bigger than they'd been yesterday? He liked to consider himself a connoisseur of that particular part of Kelsey's anatomy, but maybe it was just her bra.

*Either way, he wasn't complaining.*

"Here. My gift for Emma. And you, I hope."

She nibbled on her bottom lip, and it was only his surprise at her handing over a single sheet of glossy paper that drew his thoughts away from taking that lip between his own teeth.

He glanced down at it, and the grin that spread across his face hit before the reality of what he was looking at did.

"Is this—?" he asked.

"It is."

He hugged her, but made sure not to crush her too close—even though all he wanted to do was spin her in circles, laughing until they were both too dizzy to walk.

"When?"

"Next summer. Are you happy?"

Liam pressed his lips to hers and nodded. His stomach was all butterflies, and his heart was full enough that he'd worry it would explode if he medically didn't know better.

*Was he happy? God, had he ever been happier? That was the real question.*

"Yes, my love. I'm happy. And Emma will be, too. Think how bossy she'll be with a sibling."

They both laughed.

"I love you so much," he said. "And now I only have one request for you, Dr. Gaines."

"Name it."

"Let me make you as happy as I am right now for the rest of our lives?"

"Well, Dr. Everson, I think I can manage that."

When Liam kissed Kelsey this time, he knew with absolute certainty that his life was everything he'd ever hoped it could be. And as they celebrated their growing family, he was nothing short of grateful for the second chance he'd been given.

\* \* \* \* \*